SLIDING HOME

Contents

James Lorimer & Company Ltd., Publishers acknowledges funding support
from the Ontario Arts Council (OAC), an agency of the Government
of Ontario. We acknowledge the support of the Canada Council for the
Arts, which last year invested $153 million to bring the arts to Canadians
throughout the country. This project has been made possible in part by
the Government of Canada and with the support of the Ontario Media
Development Corporation.

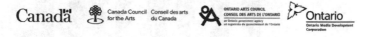

Cover design: Shabnam Safari
Cover image: Shutterstock

978-1-4594-1286-6
eBook also available 978-1-4594-1285-9

Cataloguing data available from Library and Archives Canada.

Published by:
James Lorimer & Company Ltd.,
Publishers
117 Peter Street, Suite 304
Toronto, ON, Canada
M5V 0M3
www.lorimer.ca

Distributed by:
Lerner Publisher Services
1251 Washington Ave N
Minneapolis, MN, USA
55401
www.lernerbooks.com

Printed and bound in Canada.
Manufactured by Friesens Corporation in Altona, Manitoba,
Canada in December 2017.
Job # 239693

SLIDING HOME

JOYCE GRANT

James Lorimer & Company Ltd., Publishers
Toronto

For WTW — my home team

1 TAGGED OUT

Miguel had a big problem. It was standing ninety feet away from him.

Sebastian, his teammate on the Toronto Blues, was on first base.

Miguel hitched his bat higher in the air. He circled it above his right shoulder.

He looked down the baseline. Even from that far away, Sebastian looked huge — stocky and slow. *And lazy*, thought Miguel.

Miguel knew he could hit a line drive off the pitcher. But when he did, could Sebastian stay ahead of him around the bases?

The ball came in soft and low, easy to hit. Miguel swung at it, hard. The ball soared off his bat. Then it dropped like a rock in the outfield. The Red Hawks' fielders scrambled to pick it up and throw it in.

Both runners took off from their bases.

Sebastian was like a freight train. He took awhile to

get going but once he did, you wouldn't want to get in his way.

Miguel quickly rounded first and looked to see where the ball was. He couldn't track it, but his coach was windmilling his arms. So Miguel kept running. He reached second base easily and started for third. Halfway there, he heard his coach yelling.

"Stop! *Back!*"

Sebastian hadn't gone home. The freight train had stopped at third.

Miguel was glad no one could hear what he said under his breath. He wheeled around, twisting his body. He had to get back to second base. With two out, a rundown — getting stuck between second and third base — would be disastrous for the Blues.

And it was.

"Look out! Get back!"

Miguel dodged the first tag in the rundown. But the Red Hawks' second baseman tossed the ball to third and pushed Miguel back. The ball got behind Miguel again. He pushed off the baseline toward third to avoid the tag again.

"Go home!" Miguel screamed at Sebastian. He wanted Sebastian to take home while the other team was distracted by his rundown. But the stocky boy didn't move.

And then Miguel felt the ball being pressed into his back.

"He's out!" yelled the umpire.

Silence surrounded Miguel on the long walk from second base to the dugout. The silence drowned out the cheers of the excited Red Hawks celebrating their win.

It was the Blues' third loss in a row.

"Boy, I can't wait until Jock gets back, eh?" said Sebastian, as they packed up their things.

"It wasn't Jock's fault we lost this game," said Miguel, his jaw tight.

"No, but it sure didn't help. Tami! When does he get back from the States?" Sebastian asked their first-base player.

"I don't know," Tami replied. "But I'm sick of losing to the stupid Hawks. We should have beaten them! Easily!"

"Hey, you wanna go to Pits Pita?" Sebastian asked Miguel.

"Huh?" Miguel stopped stuffing his equipment into his baseball bag. "Oh. Uh, sorry, no. I can't."

"You're mad at me," said Sebastian.

"What, because of the play? I was. But hey, it's over."

"You just said it: We didn't lose because Jock was away. You think we lost because I was too slow," said Sebastian.

Miguel wished he had time to sit around talking about things like that. He wished he could go out after a game and grab a pita. He wished his life was more like Sebastian's — more fun. And more carefree. But it wasn't.

Miguel threw his heavy baseball bag over his shoulder. He pulled out his mother's cell phone. It was old, but he was happy to have it. Its calendar kept track of all his appointments and jobs.

See you at 8. Kids have been fed. Their bedtime snack is in the fridge.

The text was from the dad of the kids he was baby-sitting that night. The screen was so scratched Miguel could barely read it.

He texted back:

KK, see you in half an hour.

What a way to spend a Friday night, thought Miguel. At least he didn't have to look after his little sister, Claudia, as well. She was at home with his mother. Looking after two kids was enough.

Miguel trudged up the steep hill to the subway. As he pushed open the heavy door to Christie Station, he heard his teammates chatting and laughing on their way to the pita restaurant.

2 BIG NEWS

Two days later, the Blues were back at Christie Pits for a practice.

One of Sebastian's arms flung out and clipped Miguel on the ear. "Ow!" Miguel glared at Sebastian.

"Sorry," said Sebastian. He ducked to avoid getting hit back.

The Blues strolled briskly back and forth in a pack. They waved their arms and brought their knees up to their chests. *We look like a flock of seagulls*, Miguel thought.

Coach Coop called out the warm-up drill. "Karaokes! One leg crosses in front of the other one."

The teammates all turned sideways, in perfect unison.

This season, Miguel had to practise even harder. He was pitching, along with the regular pitchers, Jock and Raj.

But he was also a fast base-runner. "Get on base any way you can," the coach had told him. "A walk, hit-by-pitch, line drive, bunt . . . I don't care, just get on base."

Once Miguel made it to first base, he was almost sure to get all the way around to home.

Unless, he thought, *there's someone in front of me who runs like a slug.*

He could think of one player who fit that description.

Miguel was running out in front of the others as they "ran poles." They ran from the big metal fence pole out in left field to the one on the other side, four times. Even in the hot sun, Miguel was barely breaking a sweat.

Not Sebastian.

"You look like you've been swimming, Sebastian," teased Raj.

"Gross!" said Gnash. "Look at your cap."

The band around Sebastian's blue baseball cap had turned navy. It was stuck on his wet forehead. The navy was outlined by a jagged line of white made by the salt from his sweat.

"Look at me, I'm a windmill!" Sebastian called out, spinning his arms.

Miguel was on his way back from his final pole. As he passed Sebastian, who still had one to go, he grimaced. Miguel didn't dislike the catcher. But he didn't find Sebastian's antics very funny, either.

"I don't have time for your stupid jokes," he

muttered. These days, he needed to spend every minute of his time getting things done.

Miguel waited in the dugout for the rest of the teammates to finish their poles. He reached inside Sebastian's baseball bag and found the water jug. He flipped up the lid to peer inside. He knew it — the jug was empty.

Miguel picked up his own bottle and carefully poured some water into Sebastian's jug. When the rest of the Blues arrived at the dugout, Miguel could see Sebastian's eyes narrow. He knew Sebastian was wondering what Miguel was doing with his water jug.

Miguel handed it to him. "Here. You need to hydrate." Sebastian took a big gulp. "Thanks," he said. Miguel doubted that the bigger boy even realized he'd run out of water.

"Planning ahead isn't your best thing, is it?"

Sebastian shrugged.

Lin and Tami, the only two girls on the team, arrived at the dugout drenched in sweat.

"Anyone got a granola bar?" asked Tami. She always seemed to be hungry.

"No time to eat!" said Coop. "Out onto the field for long toss."

Coop was the Blues' coach. Miguel didn't know how old Coop was, but the team thought of him more like a big kid than an adult. When Coop was thirteen, he had helped his own team to victory as a pitcher in the Summer Games. That impressed the Blues players. That and his legendary Mario Kart high score, which none of the kids could get near.

Last season Coop had sported a faux hawk. But over the winter he'd let his hair grow out — including on his face.

"Nice hipster beard," Sebastian had joked at their first glimpse of the coach's new look. "You got a new girlfriend or something?"

"Please, no! We couldn't handle another tragic break-up!" said Tami.

Miguel was back on the field first. Tami sprinted out too. The rest of the team joined them, lining up in pairs a few feet away from each other. Each one threw and caught the ball, and then took a step back to widen the distance from their partner.

Tami threw a long toss to Miguel. It hit his glove in one of its many thin spots.

"Ouch!" Miguel whipped off his glove and shook his hand in the air. "Crap!"

He rubbed his hand and wedged it back into the glove. Then he tossed the ball back to Tami. It bounced twice before it got to her. In one quick motion, Tami scooped it up and threw it hard and straight back to Miguel.

"Hey, let's move in a little," said Miguel. He took a few steps forward. He shook his hand again.

Tami was easygoing. She was happy to go along

with Miguel's suggestion. She moved toward him and got ready to throw the ball again.

Miguel cringed at the thought of another painful catch. But before Tami could throw the ball, the coach rounded up the team.

"Let's bring it in!" shouted Coop. "Come on, everyone!"

Miguel joined the crowd. Like the other players, he went down on one knee in a semi-circle in front of the coach.

"Okay. You've all heard the rumours," said Coop. "And now I can confirm . . ."

Coop didn't even get to finish his sentence before the Blues broke into cheers.

"Hey, settle down!" said the coach. "Anyway, it's all set. We are definitely going to the tournament in Ottawa."

No one seemed to notice that Miguel wasn't cheering.

3 CHARITY CASE

"Ottawa! Awesome!" said Sebastian. He punched Tami in the arm. She smiled and punched him back — slightly harder.

Sebastian rubbed his arm, but his smile said it all. An away tournament! Just what the team needed. "We'll be playing some of the best teams in the province," said Sebastian.

This was the team's first away tournament. Now that they were old enough, they would finally get to travel.

"When do we leave, Coach?" asked Tami.

"In three weeks," said Coop. "We have one game on the Friday and at least two more on the Saturday. If we do really well, we won't be home in time for dinner on Sunday."

"Good!" said Gnash. "I hate Sunday dinner."

Sebastian looked at him in surprise. "Geez. I can't think of a dinner I hate," he said. "No, wait — *tofurkey*. My cousin served that once at Thanksgiving. She's a vegan. That thing was made of *tofu*! It just isn't right."

"The trip is in three weeks?" Miguel interrupted before Sebastian could continue his bitter rant about tofu.

"Yep. Since that Friday is a PA day, we can leave Thursday after school. Our first game is at 9 a.m. on Friday."

Miguel mentally ticked off the weeks. This week he had three babysitting jobs, and every night he had to look after Claudia after school. The next week he was going to see the lawyer with his mother so he could translate. And the week after that, two more babysitting jobs. Plus, he got paid to walk a kid in his neighbourhood to daycare every morning. On the weekend of the tournament, he already had several jobs booked, plus his regular ones. His heart sank. He knew there was no way he could go on the trip.

Miguel watched his teammates high-five each other.

He wondered what it would be like to be able to take off for three days to play baseball. No work, no one to take care of. Being totally free. Never mind having money for a hotel room and restaurant dinners. He couldn't imagine it.

Sebastian saw Miguel's serious face and laughed. "Oh, man! You're bummed because Coop put us in the same hotel room, aren't you?" Sebastian had already read the page of travel details that Coop was handing out.

"Yeah, that would really suck," said Miguel. He

didn't want anyone to know how disappointed he was. Coop handed him a piece of paper, which Miguel folded and slipped into his back pocket.

He didn't even look at it. There was no need.

★ ★ ★

The next day kicked off United Way Week at Mid-Toronto Public School, where most of the Blues were in Grade 8. Groups of students had set up tables to raise money for the charity.

Sebastian was at the bake table buying a cupcake topped with a huge blob of pink icing. He held it in front of his face and eyed it greedily before shoving as much of it as he could into his mouth. Beside him, Tami was doing the same thing.

"Oh man, Miguel," said Tami through a mouthful of vanilla and sugar. "You've *gotta* try one of these!"

"No way," said Miguel. "I'm getting an empanada."

"An empa-*what*-a?" mumbled Sebastian. Miguel could clearly see the icing and cake covering his teeth.

"Oh, *gross*, Sebastian!" said Lin, giving him a shove. "At least swallow before you talk!"

Sebastian shovelled pink icing from the sides of his face back into his mouth. Then he licked his fingers, one at a time.

"Gross!" Lin repeated. She walked away.

Miguel bought a half-moon-shaped meat pastry

from the bake table. He took a big bite.

"Mmmm," he said, as he chewed. "Not as good as the ones at our family's bakery back home. But not bad. Not bad at all."

"Hey, that looks good," said Sebastian. "Let me try a bite."

Miguel broke off a piece and gave it to Sebastian. "I thought you just had dessert."

"What, the cupcake? That was an appetizer!" he said. "Hey! This is really good!"

"Told you," said Miguel.

The bell rang. The students scattered, heading for their classes. Sebastian dropped a dollar into the jar on the bake table and grabbed an empanada.

"It's a long walk to math class," he said, taking a big bite. "Don't want to get hungry!"

Miguel stopped by a table staffed by the gym teachers. A sign on the table said: Workouts, $2.

"Sebastian, that's what you need," said Miguel. "Especially after a cupcake and an empanada!"

"Two cupcakes," said Sebastian, grinning. "I got here early."

Lin and Tami turned to see why the boys had stopped.

"I would totally chip in to get Sebastian sweating," said Lin. She pulled a five-dollar bill out of her coat pocket. "Can we watch him?" she asked the gym teacher. "To make sure he actually does it?"

"I'm in!" said Tami. She tossed a handful of

change on the table. "There! That's enough for three workouts for Sebastian!"

"Hey!" said Sebastian. "Do I get a say in this?"

"No!" the others said in unison.

"Can you throw in an extra workout for free?" Miguel asked the gym teacher. He handed over a fistful of coins. "Buy five, get one free? It's for a good cause. I don't mean the United Way, I mean the *Blues*."

"You've only bought four workouts," said the gym teacher, counting the money on the table.

They turned to Sebastian, who was picking his teeth with his fingernail. When he saw everyone staring at him he stopped mid-pick.

"What?" he said. "I just spent all my money on cupcakes!"

"Oh, geez, Sebastian!" said Lin, laughing. "Okay, Tami, you and I will chip in another dollar each! You owe us, Sebastian!"

"Owe you for what?" said Sebastian, looking hurt. "For calling me a fat slob?"

"You're not fat, Sebastian," said Tami.

"No!" said Lin. She was quick to rise to their friend's defence. "Not at all!"

"Just lazy," said Miguel. "Very lazy!"

"Extremely lazy. Sooooo lazy," said Lin.

"Well, yes, that is true," said Sebastian, nodding. "So what makes you think I'll actually go to this workout thing? It's in the morning before school, right? You know how I like my sleep!"

The gym teacher looked Sebastian up and down. "You're probably, what, a catcher?" he asked.

"That's right," said Sebastian.

"You're already powerful," he said. "I can tell that by looking at you. But did you know that one of the most important things for a catcher is fast footwork? I played baseball in college — I know a ton of great drills for catchers. Plyometrics, that's what you need!"

"Plyo —" began Sebastian, looking confused.

He was cut off by the late bell for class. Miguel grabbed the workout coupons and thrust them into Sebastian's hand. "Here!" he said. The teammates scrambled, breaking into a run to get to class.

"Sebastian, you'd better go to those workouts!" Miguel shouted over his shoulder. "I don't want to be hung up at second because of you ever again!"

"See, I knew it! I knew that was still bugging you!" called Sebastian.

"I'm booking you for next Monday morning before school! North gym!" the gym teacher hollered down the hall to Sebastian. "We'll work on your footwork. And thanks for supporting the United Waaaaaay!"

4 FRAYED LEATHER

The next afternoon, the Blues were back at Christie Pits, their home away from home.

Miguel loved the place. He knew it was named Christie Pits for two reasons. First, it was shaped like a giant mixing bowl — a huge scoop out of the ground, with steeply sloping sides. A gigantic pit. Second, Coach Coop had told Miguel it had started out as a gravel pit. Now it was a beautiful park in the middle of Toronto. It had three baseball diamonds, a big soccer field, a hockey rink, a big swimming pool, basketball courts and a playground.

"There's history in this ballpark," Coach Coop would say. Looking toward the "big" diamond used by the Intercounty Baseball League, he told Miguel, "People have been playing in the Pits for decades. This is where I learned to play baseball. This park gets in your blood. It's home."

Now, at thirteen, the Blues were finally old enough to play on the big diamond. It had rough wooden bleachers for the crowd, and sometimes the local TV station covered the games.

"Getting to play on this diamond kills me, every time," Tami said as the team warmed up before their game.

"I know," said Miguel. "It's awesome."

Miguel had been eyeing the big diamond for a long time. It felt like a reward for their hard work over the years. Miguel understood hard work. He knew a lot less about rewards.

"Is that a new infield glove, Sebastian?" Miguel asked during warm-up.

"Yeah," said Sebastian.

"When did you get it?"

"Last weekend. My dad and I were in a sports store."

"But your old one is still good. And you don't even play infield!"

Sebastian turned his glove over and looked at it. "I know." He shrugged. "I like gloves. I sort of collect them, I guess."

Miguel felt his face grow hot and red. He whipped the ball to Lin.

"Ow!" said Lin, shaking her hand. "Not so hard! This is just warm-up!"

"Sorry," said Miguel as he caught her return throw. He looked over at Sebastian. And then he looked at his own glove. One of the laces had been repaired with a bit of shoelace. Even the shoelace had started to fray. Miguel tugged at the lace.

"You collect gloves," said Miguel, softly so Sebastian couldn't hear him. "Must be nice." He threw the ball.

"Ow!" said Lin, again. "Miguel!"

Coach Coop called to the team. "Okay, everyone! C'mon in!"

The Parkhill Pirates had been warming up on the other side of the diamond. Now they gathered in the visitor dugout along the first baseline.

The gravel crunched as Miguel and the Blues crossed the third baseline. They fanned out to take their places on the big diamond. Raj was the team's starting pitcher while Jock was out of town. Raj set up on the mound and threw five warm-ups. Then he threw his first pitch, hard and low. Too low.

There was no sound from the umpire as the ball scraped the dirt in front of the plate. No news was bad news — silence from the umpire almost always meant "ball."

Things got noisier for the second pitch, but only because the batter smacked it hard up the middle. The ball flew between Miguel and Tami. Gnash charged at it from centre field, picking it up gracefully and throwing it to Raj to stop the runner at first.

"Hey, Miguel!"

Miguel saw Coach Coop waving his arm in a wide arc, trying to get his attention.

"Hey! Move over!" Coop shouted.

The coach motioned for Miguel to move closer to second base. *Why would he do that?* Miguel wondered. He looked around.

"*Move!*" Sebastian shouted. Miguel didn't move. He didn't take orders from his catcher.

But Coop waved his arm, agreeing with Sebastian. Miguel trudged two steps over.

"A bit more!" shouted Coop.

Miguel moved one more step.

"Good!"

Miguel squinted at the second batter in the box. She was a strong right-hander. With a runner already on first, Miguel knew he *had* to field the ball if she got a hit. The Blues couldn't afford to let anyone get into scoring position. Not this early in the game. And not without Jock there to make a miracle play to save the day.

Miguel thought she would likely hit the ball between first and second. Now he felt too close to second base. Miguel itched to move closer to first.

"Stay there!" called Coop, who had noticed Miguel leaning back toward first.

"But . . . *righty-shift*, coach," complained Miguel. But he didn't stray.

Raj pitched a hard fastball past the batter. "Strike!" yelled the umpire.

But then — "Going! *He's GOING!*"

All the Blues in the dugout and their parents in the

stands called out at the top of their voices. The runner was taking off from first.

"Second! *Second!*" yelled Sebastian. He jumped to his feet and fired the ball. It was a bullet, hard and low, near the dirt.

Miguel was much closer to second base than he would have been if he hadn't listened to Coop. He easily moved into place to catch Sebastian's perfect throw.

Miguel's back foot hit the third-base side of second base. Just as Coop had taught him, he planted his front foot in front of the base. Then, he pivoted and trapped the ball neatly in his glove more than a second before the runner slid right into it.

"Out!" said the umpire, his fist raised.

Miguel gave Sebastian a 'nice throw' nod.

Sebastian rolled his eyes. Miguel knew it meant 'I told you so.'

Even before the batter had stepped into the box, Sebastian had known what the play would be. It wasn't about the batter at all. It was about the steal to second. That's the play Coop and Sebastian had been getting Miguel in position for. And it had worked.

"*Hunh,*" said Miguel to himself.

★ ★ ★

The game ended in a scoreless tie.

"Just do what I say next time," Sebastian said to Miguel, in the dugout.

"But how did you know?" asked Miguel. "How'd you know the runner was going to steal?"

"We've played against that kid at least two dozen times," said Sebastian. "He's their lead-off hitter. He's their fastest runner. I knew he was going to go for it. And their second batter is really strong. It was obvious."

"Yeah . . . I guess," said Miguel.

"Hey, Sebastian." Raj ruffled the catcher's hair. "How come you're so smart at baseball, and so dumb at school?"

"Hey!" said Sebastian. He pulled away from the tall pitcher and shoved him. "I'm not dumb at school!"

"Well, okay. But in comparison. I mean you're like, a freakin' genius at baseball, man!"

"Yeah," agreed Tami. "You're kind of Einstein-y at baseball."

Miguel watched the scene with interest. This was a different side of Sebastian, one he'd never seen before. A smart side. A competent side.

"*Hunh!*" he said again.

Raj shoved Sebastian playfully. "Hey, Einstein, you still coming to the movie with us tonight?"

"Of course!" said Sebastian. "We're all going, right?"

Miguel didn't say anything.

5 LOST AND FOUND

"Twirl me again!" yelled the small boy. He held his arms up to Miguel.

The Blues had gone to the movies after the game. All except for Miguel. He had stayed at the Pits. But not at the ball diamond. He was at the playground.

Miguel turned and smiled at the boy. "Okay, Alejandro," he said. "Let's go."

Miguel grabbed the boy's arms and spun him gently in a big circle. The boy's legs flung out in the air as Miguel twirled him around. Then Miguel set him neatly down on the ground. Giggling, the boy tried to walk. But he could only wobble on his feet. Then he sank dizzily to the ground.

"Me too! Me too!" A little girl about the same age as Alejandro held her arms up to Miguel.

"Okay, Claudia — you too," said Miguel.

Miguel was on his knees, talking to the giggling children, when he heard voices he knew.

"Hey, Miguel!" said Raj.

Lost and Found

Raj was in a pack with the rest of the Blues, coming down the path toward the playground.

"Oh man, you missed a great movie!" said Lin.

"Yeah, you should have seen it," said Sebastian. "There was this one crazy chase . . ."

"Again, again!" said Alejandro. He held his arms up to Miguel. "Again!"

"Sorry, guys," said Miguel to his teammates. He bent down to pick up the little boy.

"What's going on?" asked Gnash. "Is this your brother or something?"

"I'm working," said Miguel. "I can't talk right now."

"I'm his sister! I'm Claudia," said the girl. She walked right up to Sebastian.

"Babysitting?" asked Sebastian.

"Come on, guys," said Gnash to the others. "Let's leave him alone. The man is just trying to earn a living!"

Gnash winked at Miguel and roughly shoved the others off toward the swings.

"Don't listen to them, man," he said to Miguel. "Most of them have never held down a job in their lives. They don't know what it's like to be a working stiff like us!" The season before, Gnash had missed several games because of work. Miguel knew he had a job in the corner store near his apartment.

"Thanks," said Miguel. He brought Claudia a bucket and shovel to make castles in the sand pit.

Alejandro jumped up and down in front of Miguel.

Miguel picked up the little boy and twirled him until he was giggling and dizzy again. Then he set him down gently on the sand. The boy began to take a step, but lurched forward to his knees.

"Whoa!" said Sebastian, reaching out to steady the boy. Then he laughed. "You're so dizzy!"

"Alejandro, this is Sebastian," said Miguel. "Sebastian, meet Alejandro."

The boy was still giggling. But he managed to thrust out one small hand toward Sebastian, as Miguel had taught him.

"Sebastian plays baseball," he said. He saw the boy's eyes grow wide. "He's a catcher."

"Wow!" said Alejandro. "I play baseball, too!"

"You do?" asked Sebastian. He crouched down to the boy's level. "What position do you play?"

The boy looked up at Miguel.

"You're a utility player," Miguel explained with a smile. "You can play any position."

"Yeah!" said Alejandro. "I can play any position!"

"Sebastian is an awesome catcher," Miguel told Alejandro.

"He's good?" Claudia asked.

"Best I've ever seen," said Miguel.

Sebastian looked surprised. "Are you sure you should be lying to the kids?" he asked.

"What are you talking about?" asked Miguel.

"You're a really good catcher!"

"I know that. But I didn't think you did," said Sebastian. "I also know that you don't like me."

"Oh, geez, Sebastian," said Miguel. "Stop it. I like you."

"Then why don't you want to room with me in Ottawa? And why do you never come with us to the movies or anywhere? And how come you always take off right after school? Because you don't like us, that's why. You don't like me."

Miguel rolled his eyes. "I'm busy!" he said. "I have to do stuff. Like babysit —"

He broke off suddenly and looked around the playground.

"Oh no!" he said.

"What?" asked Sebastian.

"Alejandro! He's gone! *Alejaaaaaaaandro!*" Miguel called. He felt panic begin to work its way up into his throat.

Miguel and Sebastian walked around the playground. They checked under and over every piece of equipment, looking for the small boy.

"Alejaaaaaaaandro!" Miguel called.

Miguel heard his teammates calling for Alejandro as well.

"Found him!" said Gnash, near the splash pad. He was frantically waving Miguel over.

"Here!" came a small voice, finally. "I'm here!"

Miguel ran over to the splash pad. There, in the middle of the water, his pants soaked past his knees, was Alejandro.

"Alejandro!" cried Miguel, wading in. He crouched down and looked in the boy's eyes. "You must never run away from me!"

"I was just —"

"No!" said Miguel. "You stay with me and Claudia, okay? We all stay together!"

The boy nodded slowly, his eyes wide. He held out his hand to Miguel, who took it in his and led him out of the splash pad. Sebastian, holding Claudia's hand, was watching from the edge.

"I can't talk to you right now, Sebastian," said Miguel. "I need to focus on these guys. Sorry."

"Okay," said Sebastian. He handed Claudia over to Miguel.

"So . . . this work stuff is *serious*," he said quietly.

Sebastian patted Alejandro lightly on the head and walked off to join the rest of the Blues. They were going down the slide on their bellies at stupid speeds. Smaller kids in the playground leaped out of the way as the baseball players barrelled toward them.

Miguel smoothed down a lock of Alejandro's hair.

"Wanna play on the swings?" he asked the children.

"Okay!"

6 WORKOUT BUDDIES

"Have a good day, sweetheart," Miguel's mother said to him in Spanish. She put his lunch in his backpack and zipped it up. "Don't forget we have to see the lawyer tonight. So come right home after school."

"I know, Mama, I know," said Miguel. He gave his mother a peck on the cheek and headed out the door with Claudia. They went down the block to a house with a red door. They turned up the walkway, which was strewn with tricycles and toys.

Before Miguel could knock, the door opened. Miguel and Claudia were greeted by a chattering Alejandro and his mother.

"Thanks for dropping him off," she said in Spanish, handing Miguel an envelope. "Good morning, Claudia!"

"No problem," said Miguel. He waved the envelope in thanks and took Alejandro's hand.

"Morning, Alejandro," he said to the boy. Miguel carefully folded the envelope full of babysitting money and tucked it into his back pocket.

Miguel enjoyed the stream of happy chatter all the way to the nursery school, which was attached to his own middle school. He made sure Alejandro and Claudia had everything they needed for the day, and were safely in the hands of their teachers. Then he said goodbye and set off toward the school library.

Crossing the lobby, he noticed a familiar figure.

"Sebastian!" he said. He was surprised to see his teammate at school so early.

"Miguel!" said Sebastian.

And then Miguel remembered. "You're going to a workout, aren't you?"

"Yep," said Sebastian. "I've been going all week."

"How are they going?" asked Miguel.

"Watch this," said Sebastian. He put down his backpack and started running in place, pumping his knees up high. Then he leaped sideways back and forth, as though dodging an imaginary line.

"Impressive footwork," said Miguel. "You do seem slightly more . . . well, less . . ."

"I am!" said Sebastian, finishing off his move. "I'm getting super-fast."

"That's great," said Miguel, nodding.

"But what are *you* doing here?"

"I had to drop Alejandro and Claudia off at daycare."

"Wow, you had to get up this early?" Sebastian looked shocked. "That's horrible!"

"I do it every day." Miguel shrugged.

"Every day? Like, every . . . day? You're always here at this time?"

"Yep."

"But it's not even eight o'clock! What do you do until school starts?"

"Homework. I don't have time to finish it after school, anyway."

"Oh geez!" Sebastian looked so shocked, Miguel had to laugh.

And then Sebastian's face brightened. "Hey, why don't you come with me now?"

"Where?"

"The gym. I'm sure the coach will let you try the drills." He looked at the clock on the wall. "C'mon," he said. "We can't be late!"

Smiling, Miguel trailed after him. Sebastian was practically running down the hallway toward the gym. Miguel had never seen Sebastian worry about being late for anything.

"Good morning!" said the gym teacher, when the two boys burst into the gym, puffing. "Here, give me a hand!"

Miguel took the long, thin rope the teacher handed him. It was tied into a ladder that they stretched out on the floor. Off to one side of the gym, Sebastian was laying out a row of orange cones.

"Okay, Sebastian," said the teacher. He looked at

Miguel. "Are you going to do the drills too?"

"He's on my baseball team, Sir," said Sebastian. "The Blues."

Miguel had never heard his teammate speak with such respect to a teacher. Sebastian had always seemed like a likeable goofball with no respect for authority.

The teacher blew a whistle and the two boys fell into line. "Go!" said the teacher.

Miguel watched Sebastian run the "ladder," his knees coming up hard on each step.

"Faster!" called the teacher. "Faster! Pump those knees!"

Sebastian was doing a good job, but Miguel was able to do the drills faster. On his turn, he flew across the rungs, his knees up high. The boys took three turns each. When they were done, Sebastian's face was dripping with sweat.

"You don't even look . . . like you've . . . been running," Sebastian puffed. He was bent over and his hands were on his knees. His belly was heaving in and out.

"No time to rest, guys," said the coach. "Quickly! Over here."

The next drill was speed hurdles. Each boy ran over six small hurdles, about a foot high.

"Faster!" said the gym teacher. "Again!"

After that, the teacher had the boys go into a crouch. They had to jump up quickly and then fake a throw.

"This is to improve my pop-time," explained Sebastian.

"What's that?" asked Miguel, panting.

"As soon as I catch the ball, I need to be able to jump up and throw it to the player on base. This helps me be more explosive. It's called plyometrics!"

The boys worked hard for forty-five minutes, until the coach blew his whistle.

"Okay! Good work today!" He turned to Sebastian. "Great job." He thumped Sebastian on his sweat-soaked back. "You're going to be fierce this season."

Sebastian's face was red and blotchy. "I'm not as fast as Miguel," he said.

"Not yet," said the coach. "But you will be."

It was clear from the boys' faces that neither of them really believed that.

"He will," the coach said again. "I've seen it a million times. It's just a different running style. Sebastian, you've got long legs. Miguel's centre of gravity is closer to the ground, so he runs differently. You'll catch up to him. You'll see."

They put away the cones and hurdles until the bell rang to start class.

"So," said Sebastian as they were leaving. "You want to get something to eat after school?"

Miguel thought about the appointment he had with his mother that afternoon to see Mr. Raymond, their lawyer.

"I can't," he said. He saw Sebastian's face fall.

"Right," said Sebastian.

Sebastian turned away before Miguel could respond.

"I've got to get to class," snapped Sebastian. He strode out of the gym.

7 STOMACH ACHE

"I don't understand," said Mrs. Estrada in Spanish. She squinted at the paper on the oak desk in front of her.

"Well, Mrs. Estrada, there are still some papers that need to be filed to complete your sponsorship of your husband from El Salvador . . ."

Mrs. Estrada looked from Mr. Raymond to Miguel as he translated the lawyer's words. "What papers?" she asked her son.

"They're saying that Dad's application to come to Canada isn't complete," Miguel told his mother in Spanish. "There was a mix-up with some of the papers we filed."

Miguel saw his mother's eyes cloud with worry.

"Nothing serious," Miguel added quickly. "I just need to redo a couple of forms. And then you'll need to sign them."

Mr. Raymond waited patiently while the two spoke in Spanish. He nodded and said, "That's right."

Miguel's mother tucked a strand of hair behind her

ear. Miguel took one of the glasses on the tray in front of him and poured his mother a glass of water. He slid it over to her.

"Ask him how soon we can refile the papers," Miguel's mother urged, in Spanish.

Miguel repeated the question in English.

"Fairly quickly," said Mr. Raymond. "We are going to make sure it happens as fast as possible. A few weeks at the most."

Miguel's mother tugged at her hair again. She took a long drink of water.

"Okay, thank you," she said in English. She stood and held out her hand to the lawyer. "You do understand that it is . . . urgent?"

"Yes, I understand," Mr. Raymond said.

Miguel and his mother had explained that life in El Salvador had become much more dangerous for Mr. Estrada. The bakery he ran had attracted the attention of a dangerous gang. Three of them had come by. They said that if they weren't given a large sum of money, "something bad might happen" to the bakery. It was their family's main source of income.

Something bad, thought Miguel, *like an "accidental" fire*. That's what had happened to his aunt's tailor shop. She had run out of money to pay the gangs. The next week, her precious sewing machines and fabrics had gone up in flames.

"The sooner we can get him out of El Salvador and

away from those . . ." Miguel's mother looked at him.

"Tell your mom to try not to worry too much," Mr. Raymond said to Miguel. His eyes were kind. "Your dad will be here before you know it."

Outside the lawyer's office, Miguel's mother turned to him. "I thought we had already filed all the papers!" she said in Spanish.

"It might have been my fault," said Miguel. He put one hand on his stomach. "Maybe I messed up the English."

"Oh, Miguel." She dropped her bag on the ground and reached for him. Pulling him into a tight hug she said, "You did nothing wrong."

"You don't know that," said Miguel. "I should ask Mr. Raymond. Maybe it's my fault that Daddy isn't here already."

"It wasn't your fault," she said firmly. "You've been so helpful! I don't know what we would have done without you." She zipped up his jacket and put a hand on his shoulder. "Don't worry," she told her son. "We will get our family together again. We will do whatever it takes." Then she smiled. "Now, how about a freezie?" She gestured toward the corner store.

Miguel managed a feeble smile. "Sounds good," he said.

Miguel's mother put her arm around him and pulled him close. "It will work out," she said softly. "Don't worry. Now let's get Claudia from Alejandro's.

I'll make us a nice dinner. Maybe we'll Skype Daddy tonight."

But Miguel did worry. Unless they could bring his father to Canada soon, something terrible might happen. They had left him in El Salvador three years before. Since then, all they talked about was getting everyone back together again.

Recently, the violence had become worse in their old neighbourhood. Miguel's father had always given the gang *protection money*. "Protection against themselves," Miguel's mother had explained to him. "But lately they have been demanding more. More money than we could ever afford. We had some money in our savings, but now it is nearly all gone."

Miguel pictured his father in El Salvador. He loved his father. Once, he had loved his home there. But their part of town had become different — scarier. Too scary for him and Claudia. And now, it looked like it was getting too dangerous for their father, too.

Miguel was still worried that night, when he was supposed to be sleeping. And he worried as soon as he opened his eyes the next morning and his happy baseball dreams faded away.

"Ow!"

Miguel's stomach felt like it was on fire. He clutched it. He swung his legs out over the bed and put his feet on the floor. He tried to stand up, but he couldn't.

Stomach Ache

"Ow!" he moaned again. He leaned forward and dug his clenched fist into his stomach. He rocked back and forth.

He'd had the stomach ache before. He tried to think of something nice. A baseball game. Hitting a home run. But for every nice thought, a bad thought came too. He perched on the edge of his bed and waited for the pain to pass.

8 TRASH TALK

"It's been three in a row," said Tami. She grunted as she caught Jock's throw.

Jock, their best player, had finally come back from his trip. He'd been in the United States to visit some of his old friends.

"Four," Jock said.

"Three! It's been three!"

The Blues were warming up on the home side of the big diamond. They were about to face their toughest rivals, the Parkhill Pirates. They were arguing over how many times in a row they'd beaten the team.

"Look, there was the game where Gnash got tagged out," said Tami.

She was talking about a game against the Pirates the season before. The Blues had faked out their opponents by letting Gnash get tagged out on purpose. As the Pirates celebrated their "win," Jock had quietly sped past them all to steal home and score the winning run.

"Uh, yeah, Tami. I kinda remember that game," said Jock, smiling.

"And then there was the one two weeks ago with that crazy overthrow to third."

"Right."

"And after that, the game when their outfielders —" Tami suddenly started laughing. She bent over and propped her hands on her knees. She was still bent over, laughing, when Jock threw a rocket intended for her glove. It went whizzing by her. The ball clattered noisily against the metal fence.

That only made Tami laugh harder. She stood up and wiped tears of laughter from her cheeks. She tried to speak. ". . . collided . . ."

"Oh, man," said Jock, starting to chuckle. Now he understood what was so funny.

"They collided! Crashed right into each other!" Tami could barely get the words out.

"Yeah," laughed Jock. "That was a bit of a problem for them."

"And then the ball . . . just . . . *fell* . . . in between them!" Tami wiped her eyes again.

"Hey, I'm not normally one to trash talk another team," said Jock. "But even the Pirates would have to admit — that was a really awful play!"

There was no love lost between Jock and the Pirates. When they had found out Jock was gay, many of the Pirates — especially Stretch, the Pirates' first baseman — taunted and bullied him. Jock and Gnash had managed to get away from the bullies before anyone got hurt. Even a written apology by the Pirates and their coach hadn't eased tensions between the teams.

"Hey, don't be too hard on 'em," said Gnash. "Maybe the sun was in their eyes."

"That must be it," said Tami. She picked up the ball and threw it back to Jock.

"You think I should lend them my sunglasses for today's game?" asked Gnash, laughing.

"Let's just warm up, eh?" said Miguel. *Why does everyone always seem to have time for jokes?* he wondered.

The teammates threw the ball back and forth, still giggling.

"Hey, Miguel, you okay?" asked Tami. "You look like you haven't slept in four days."

"I'm fine," said Miguel tersely.

"We're talking about the last game we played against the Pirates," said Jock.

"I know. When Stretch broke his foot?" said Miguel. "Hilarious — a real riot."

"Hey!" said Jock. "See? That's four games we won!"

"No," said Tami. "Remember? *How* did Stretch break his foot?"

"Oh yeah," said Jock, his smile fading. "Tripping over those idiots in the outfield."

"Yeah, trying to get the ball," said Tami. "That was the same game."

"To be fair, we didn't find out about his foot until the next day," said Raj.

"Hey," said Tami. "Remember the Instagram pictures he posted of his gross, swollen, blue foot?"

"Yeah. He's such a delightful person," said Raj.

"I wonder if he'll be here today," said Tami.

"Who cares?" said Gnash. "The guy's a jerk."

Jock's teammates had rallied to his defence when the Pirates were being mean to him. They didn't like one of their own being bullied — even if they had done some of the bullying themselves at first. But that was before they'd gotten to know Jock. Before they had learned more about what it meant to be gay.

They broke off their talk when they heard the crunch of tires on the gravel in the parking lot. A dozen big, black SUVs pulled up, one after the other. Car doors opened and the Parkhill Pirates spilled out, a sea of bright white uniforms.

"Speak of the devil," said Gnash.

Stretch was being helped out of the car by his parents. They handed him a pair of shiny silver crutches. Stretch limped along the sidewalk at the top of the steep hill. He looked down into the Pits.

"C'mon, jump! We'll catch you!" shouted Sebastian with a big grin. He was holding out his arms as if he expected Stretch to leap into them.

Sebastian can turn anything into a joke, thought Miguel.

Sliding Home

★ ★ ★

"You look tired," said Sebastian to Miguel. The two boys were standing with Coach Coop at home plate. They waited as the umpire finished explaining the ground rules.

Ben, the tall, friendly home-plate umpire, pointed to a hole in the fence. "Anything along the fence line is in play," he said. "If a ball gets stuck under the outfield fence, put your hands up and we'll call it a dead ball. But if you reach in to get the ball, we'll assume it's in play."

"I didn't get a lot of sleep last night," said Miguel, answering Sebastian's comment.

"What, because of our workout? It wasn't so hard," said Sebastian.

"Oh, and please tell your on-deck batters to get any balls that go to the backstop if there's nobody on. The backstop is a lot bigger on this diamond," said Ben.

The boys didn't bother listening. They'd played in Christie Pits for so many years they knew every inch of every diamond.

"Hey, are you looking forward to the big trip?" asked Sebastian.

"Uh," said Miguel, looking down at the ground.

"Oh no," said Sebastian. "Don't tell me. You're not going."

"I've got to . . ." said Miguel.

"Work. I know. That's a handy excuse."

"Sebastian . . ." Miguel began.

"They're wrapping up," Sebastian cut him off. "You'd better get out there."

"Thanks, Blue," said Coach Coop, shaking the umpire's hand.

"Have a good game," said Ben. He took his position behind Sebastian at the plate.

Miguel turned and jogged to his spot at second.

On the mound, Jock was throwing warm-up pitches to Sebastian. For once, Sebastian wasn't laughing or making smart remarks.

"Second base, coming *down!*" Sebastian yelled. He fired the ball toward Miguel. The throw was high, and Miguel had to jump to catch it. He managed to get it. But his throw back to Sebastian missed the catcher's mitt by a mile.

Sebastian ripped off his mask and threw it on the ground. He sprinted to the backstop to fetch the ball. Even from second base, Miguel could hear him complaining about the throw.

Sebastian tossed the ball to Ben and took his place behind the plate.

The young umpire brought his own mask down over his face. He crouched behind Sebastian.

"Play ball!"

9 ROUGH DAY

"Look at them!" yelled Stretch from the bench in the visitor dugout. His crutches were propped beside him. They tripped his teammates as they tried to edge past to go up to bat. "They can't even catch the ball! We're gonna kill 'em! Goooo Pirates!"

Miguel saw Jock shoot a look at the visitor dugout. He watched the pitcher adjust his front foot so it was pointing straight forward. Then Jock drew the ball back and launched it at the plate. Straight and hard.

"Strike!" the umpire yelled, his fist in the air.

The Pirate at the plate, a tall right-hander named Katie, glared at Jock. She stepped back into the batter's box and loaded up for the second pitch.

"Strike!" said the umpire after Jock's second pitch.

The third pitch came in low and inside. Katie swung hard at it. Her bat caught a piece of the ball, sending it soaring up into the air. Sebastian stood up and snatched off his mask. He looked skyward, holding up his glove. The ball fell into it with a soft *thunk*.

"That's a catch!" said the umpire.

Jock strode off the mound to the dugout. Miguel gave him a high-five. "And that's how you do that, my friend," he said.

"The best way to answer jerks like the Pirates," said Jock, "is on the field. Beat them on the field."

Miguel sat down beside Jock and Raj on the bench. Stretch was still yapping loudly in the visitor dugout.

"Guys like Stretch have bugged me my whole life," said Jock.

"Yeah," said Raj.

"Ya can't change them. And anyway, that's not our job. Our job is to keep moving forward, in spite of the Stretches in this world. And focus on our own dreams."

Miguel thought about Jock's words. "But what if it's not just one guy?" he asked.

"What do you mean?" asked Raj.

"What if it's a whole bunch of guys?" asked Miguel.

"There's a bunch of guys bullying you?" asked Jock.

"Never mind," said Miguel. He got up and grabbed his bat. He walked out of the dugout.

★ ★ ★

The more Miguel thought about Jock's words, the more they made sense to him. He and his family were being bullied. Not by one person, but by a whole lot of people — the gangs. But it was more than that. Sometimes it felt like there was a whole system holding them back, stopping his father from getting out of El Salvador.

What had his parents ever done wrong? They were hard-working people. They were a close-knit family that wanted nothing more than a shot at a better life. Why was this happening to them?

Miguel could feel his stomach tighten. He tried to ignore it as he took his place at the plate. Waiting for his pitch, he could hear Stretch's nasal chirp cutting through all the other sounds of the ballpark.

"Heeeeeey, battah! Battah-battah-battah!"

Miguel swung hard at the first pitch. He missed the ball. The force of his swing brought him around in a circle. He let go of the bat with one hand. It swung around in a wide arc, nearly hitting the fence.

Miguel stepped into the box again. He watched the pitcher move the ball around in his hands. He lined up two of his fingers with the red seams on the ball. Miguel knew that meant a fastball was coming. When it came, he was ready for it.

"Comes in fast, goes out fast," he said under his breath. He watched the ball leave the pitcher's hand. It came directly toward him. He kept watching the ball until his bat made contact with it, smashing into it with a loud crack.

The ball flew off to his left, near the Pirates' third-base player. Miguel took off for first base. He flew down the baseline. He touched first base and rounded for second.

The Pirates' second baseman was yelling to the third baseman. Miguel couldn't make out what he was saying. It was probably, "Give me the ball!"

All of a sudden, it was no longer about baseball for Miguel. It was about everything. It was about his terrible morning. It was about being worried all the time. And the bakery that his father was fighting to protect. And the unfairness of being a kid who had a job. And it was about rich people.

Miguel had a sudden urge to smash through anything standing in his way. And right now, that was the guy on second base.

Out of the corner of his eye, he saw the Pirates' third baseman launch the ball to their second baseman. Miguel rose up. With a mighty lunge, he threw his feet forward. Miguel felt like he was moving in slow motion. He felt the gravelly dirt give way as the heels of his cleats carved a trench through it. His hands went up over his head. He flew, nearly horizontal, toward the base.

The Pirates' second baseman had the ball. He was in front of the base, waiting to tag him out. And then, sickeningly, he wasn't. Miguel felt the crunch of his cleats against the ankle of the Pirate. He was still sliding as the player came down on top of him with all of his weight. There was a dull thud as they collided. Miguel was still sliding. He realized in a panic that if he didn't grab the base, he was going to slide right past it. He twisted his body around and clawed at the base. He didn't want all of this to be for nothing.

Miguel managed to catch the base with his right hand. He held on to it. The umpire towered over Miguel and the Pirate. He spread his arms wide in a sweeping gesture.

"Safe!"

The crowds on both sides of the field erupted. Parents and children were yelling. Depending on which side they were on, they were screaming about how fair or unfair the call was. A few of the parents on both sides were yelling at Miguel for making a "rough slide."

Miguel barely heard any of it. He was thinking about how much he wanted to win the game. How much he wanted to beat the Pirates. At that moment, those were the only thoughts in his head.

"Time!" he called to the ump. He stood up and brushed off his pants, careful to keep one foot on the base.

That was when he noticed that the player at second base hadn't gotten up. The Pirate was trying to get up using only one leg. But he couldn't. Miguel saw that the boy's pant leg was ripped where his cleat had gone into it.

Rough Day

Miguel stopped thinking about winning. He no longer felt blinded with anger. He held a hand down to the boy to help him up.

"Get away from me!" said the second baseman, through gritted teeth. "Jerk!"

The noise of the crowd washed over Miguel, full force. He had done something terrible. Something that might have resulted in someone getting hurt. Miguel felt his face go red. But he didn't move his foot from the base.

10 OFF BASE

Coach Coop sprinted out to second base. He put his arm around Miguel. In a low voice, he said, "All right. All right. You're good." Then he went over to talk to Ben, the umpire.

Miguel couldn't hear what they were saying. The Pirates' coach was yelling something at Ben. Ben was holding up his hands and shaking his head at both coaches. The umpire took a step back from the coaches.

The Pirates' coach became more and more agitated. The umpire pointed at him, and then at the dugout. Although Miguel couldn't hear the words, it was clear that the Pirates' coach was being kicked out of the game.

Players from both sides poured out of their dugouts and onto the field. Miguel saw Gnash shove one of the Pirates. Stretch hopped onto the field on one foot, carrying one of his crutches. He was screaming and his face was beet red.

Slowly, Miguel took his foot off the base. Then, he walked right into the dugout.

Miguel watched the chaos from the bench. Ben was trying to stop the argument. But things were clearly well past anything the young umpire could do.

"Everybody, get back to your dugout," he said. He waved his arms at both teams and pointed toward their dugouts. "Get back to your dugout now or this game is over!"

Beside Miguel on the bench was Sebastian. Miguel was shocked to see that the catcher was laughing.

"Nice job!" he said.

"What?" asked Miguel.

"Are you kidding? You slid into that kid like a bulldozer. Did you see his pants?"

"I was going for the base."

"I know you were. But don't you think you were going for it a bit *hard?*"

Miguel felt his face become hot. He got up and walked back onto the field, where the others were taking their places again. The Pirates' second baseman was in the visitor dugout with ice on his ankle.

In his place was another Pirates player. Miguel nodded to her. She shoved her cap down on her head and looked away from him.

"You'd better not try that crap with me," she said. "Or you'll be sorry."

Her words sent a chill down Miguel's spine. *You'll be sorry.* It was exactly what one of the thugs had said to his father. In fact, it was one of the reasons Miguel's mother had gone on ahead with the children to Canada.

"Play ball!" Ben's voice carried to second base.

The game ended in a tie. But Miguel no longer cared about the score. He felt that he had lost. He'd lost control of his anger. He felt like he was losing his self-respect, too.

He just wanted to go home. He wanted to be held by his mother, to have her tell him that it would all be okay. He wanted to stop feeling responsible for everything. He wanted someone to say they were on his side. That he wouldn't have to work anymore, and that his father would be fine.

But he knew none of that could happen. Not yet.

As if reading his mind, Jock approached Miguel in the dugout after the game.

"I'm with you," he said simply.

Miguel stopped shoving his equipment in his bag and looked up. "What?"

"I said, I'm with you."

"What? Why?"

"Because you're a good person."

"No, I'm not," said Miguel. His voice trembled. "I nearly broke that kid's ankle."

"But you didn't," said Jock. They could see in the visitor dugout that the hurt Pirates player was up now, walking gingerly on both feet.

"But I could have."

"But you didn't," Jock repeated.

"Maybe I wanted to," said Miguel. His bottom lip quivered.

Jock put his arm around Miguel's shoulders. "No, you didn't want to," he said. "You were angry. But you're not that kind of guy. You're not someone who hurts other people."

"How do you know?"

"I know, because I know you. And I've been there. I've felt like I was under pressure to do everything. To help my mom, to get good grades. To be the best ball player. To have to stand up for everyone in the world who is gay."

Miguel was fighting to hold back tears.

"You didn't want to hurt that guy. But you're hurting. And you want it to stop. Am I right?" Jock was practically whispering now.

Miguel nodded.

"Dude, you're a good guy. You have too much going on, sure. But you're a good guy."

They were interrupted by the other Blues crashing into the fence and pouring noisily into the dugout. Gnash shoved Miguel as he went past him. "Nice job, Crusher!" he said.

"No!" said Miguel. "Don't call me that! That's horrible."

Gnash smiled at his teammate. "Hey, I meant it as a compliment!"

"That kid's going to have a nice bruise," said Tami.

"Yeah! Who knew Miguel had it in him?" asked Sebastian with a laugh.

Miguel looked from one teammate to the next. "No!" he said. "Stop it!"

"Aw, relax," said Sebastian. "It happened. You didn't mean it. But it happened. We've all done it!"

Miguel's expression showed that he didn't believe him.

"Really!" said Sebastian. "Hey, Lin, remember last year? When I smashed into that kid at home plate?"

"Yeah, catchers beating up catchers," said Lin. "Not your finest moment."

"And remember last year?" asked Gnash. "When I nearly pummelled the crap out of Jock?"

"Hey!" said Jock. "I think you mean I pummelled you!"

Jock gave Gnash a playful shove.

Coop stuck his head in the dugout and said, "Pack up. Now. Go home, everyone. We'll talk about this tomorrow." Then he rejoined the parents.

11 TRADING UP

"This piece of inari for a pupusa," said Tami.

"A whole pupusa? For one little inari? No deal," said Miguel.

The Blues were trading lunches. Tami, who loved to eat, was trying to trade up. She was trying to swap every piece of sushi she had for something bigger and better.

"My perfect lunch would include something from everyone else's," she said. So far, she had an eggroll, two small samosas and a piece of Gnash's pizza. She was trying to finish off her meal with one of Miguel's pork-and-cheese-filled pupusas.

Unlike empanadas, which were half-moon shaped and crispy, pupusas were round and soft. Miguel thought his mother made the best pupusas. "It's worth more than just one of those rice-filled tofu things," he said.

"Speaking of tofu . . . where's Sebastian?" Tami asked, looking around the lunchroom.

"He said he was going to try to get in another quick workout," said Jock.

Miguel was impressed. The catcher's new workout routine seemed to be paying off. "He's already a lot faster off the base than he used to be," said Miguel.

"Yeah, and he doesn't get all sweaty and gross when we run poles," said Lin. "Well, he still does, but he doesn't stink as much."

Sebastian came sprinting through the cafeteria and crashed into the table to join the gang. "You keep this up and you might become a real athlete, Sebastian!" said Jock.

"But I can't say the workouts are making you any more graceful," said Lin, laughing.

"What did you bring for lunch?" asked Tami. She looked at the paper sack in his hand.

"I have no idea," said Sebastian. He opened it and peered in.

Jock looked at Miguel. "Did you hear that?" he asked.

"Yeah, but I don't believe it," said Miguel.

"What?" asked Sebastian. He took a bundle of carrot sticks out of the bag and put it on the table. He pulled out some raw green beans and some ranch dip.

"You don't know what's in your lunch?" asked Jock.

"Yeah, when's the last time you didn't know what was in your lunch?" asked Tami. She picked up the carrot sticks and sniffed them.

"Hey! Give me those!" Sebastian snatched them back.

"Carrot sticks?" said Gnash, his eyes wide. "I've never seen you eat those before."

The whole table watched as Sebastian took a crunchy bite of carrot.

"Whoa!" said Lin.

"I feel like I'm looking at something no one has ever seen before. Like, like a new planet. Or a sea monster!" said Tami.

"Or a dragon being hatched . . ." agreed Gnash.

"Or a . . . miracle!" said Lin.

"Hey, am I going to have to find another table to sit at?" asked Sebastian. "Because you idiots are making me lose my appetite!"

"Well, he still has an appetite," said Miguel. "At least that's normal."

"Hey, Miguel," said Sebastian. "To change the subject — have you decided whether you're going to Ottawa with us or not?"

"Not," said Miguel.

"Oh geez. Your mom won't let you go because of what you did yesterday at the game?" asked Sebastian.

"No, it's not that," said Miguel. He pulled out his mother's phone and clicked on its calendar. He opened up the weekend of the Ottawa trip and put the phone on the table so everyone could see.

"What's 'Sit' mean?" asked Lin, pointing to a calendar entry. "There's a lot of that."

"It's his relaxing time," said Sebastian.

"It's short for babysitting," said Miguel. "Those are my babysitting jobs."

He pointed to one entry in the calendar after another. "And that's walking Claudia and Alejandro home from school on Friday — I get paid pretty well for that. And that's helping my other neighbour with her grocery shopping on Saturday morning. And I'm babysitting that night, and . . . oh, look, how wonderful. On that Sunday, I've got not one but *two* babysitting gigs."

"Miguel!" said Sebastian. "You've got something every day!"

"Yep," said Miguel.

"But you're going to have to cancel them all!" Sebastian crunched down on a carrot stick. "So you can come on the trip!"

"Nope," said Miguel.

Gnash put his hand on Sebastian's shoulder. He drew him around until he was looking him in the eye. "Miguel can't cancel his appointments," he told Sebastian. "He needs the work."

"He does?" asked Sebastian, still not getting it. "But why?"

"He. Needs. The. Money," said Gnash slowly.

"Money? Why don't you just ask your mom for some?" asked Sebastian, his eyes wide.

The teammates were now all talking over themselves, trying to get Sebastian to understand.

"I wasn't born with a silver spoon in my mouth," said Miguel. "Like some people."

"Neither was I," said Jock. "When my mom and I were living in New Jersey, she had two jobs and I had a job at the Cineplex. And we still couldn't make ends meet!"

"Rent is a lot," said Miguel. "And then there's telephone and electricity and water and . . ."

"Yeah, but why can't you afford that stuff?" asked Sebastian. "Doesn't your mom have a job?"

"When you come from another country, sometimes you have to start at the bottom," said Gnash. "Like, I know a doctor from Guatemala who drives a taxi."

"Yeah, and my friend is from Syria," said Tami. "Her mom has a degree in civil engineering. But she's working in Canada as a cleaner."

"Why?" asked Sebastian. "We need doctors here in Canada. We need . . . engineer-whatsits."

"Well, yeah," said Miguel. "But when you have a degree from one country, it's not always accepted in another one. Sometimes you have to do your schooling all over again, even though you are perfectly good at your job."

"Like my friend's dad," said Tami. "He's going to night school so he can take most of his degree over again in Canada."

"In El Salvador, my mom and dad ran a bake shop," said Miguel. "They were doing okay. But there were these bad people they had to pay so they wouldn't wreck the bakery."

"What?!" exclaimed Tami.

"Yeah, well, it gets worse," said Miguel. "Everything was okay — or relatively okay. But then the bakery started doing better. We even got some celebrities buying our stuff."

"That's good, isn't it?" asked Sebastian.

"Yeah, except then the bakery caught the attention of the really bad gangs. They started demanding more and more money. It's a long story. But basically, we ran out of our savings. And if my dad doesn't get out of the country . . ."

"That's terrible!" said Lin.

"Yeah, couldn't you just call the cops or something?" asked Sebastian.

"It's probably not that simple, is it?" asked Jock.

"No. I don't even understand it all. There's a lot of stuff my parents won't tell me. They don't want me to worry. Too late!" said Miguel, rolling his eyes.

"So is your dad going to be okay?" asked Sebastian.

"I think he is. If we can get him to Canada soon," said Miguel. "But that's really expensive. There are lawyers' fees and fees to file all the forms. Everything costs money."

Sebastian dug his hand into his paper lunch sack and came up with half an egg sandwich. He unwrapped it and bit into it.

"Man," he said. "I had no idea."

"Yeah, most people don't," said Gnash. "If you don't have money problems, you probably think no one else does."

Sebastian was still thoughtfully chewing his lunch when the bell rang. Everyone got up from the table.

"Hey, Miguel," said Sebastian, as they walked out of the cafeteria together.

"Yeah?"

"Do you want a carrot stick?"

He held one out.

"Sure," said Miguel, taking it.

12 MUDBALL!

From his bed the next morning, Miguel could hear the sharp *tick, tick, tick* of raindrops on the roof outside his window. Rain. That meant baseball practice would be cancelled. Whenever it rained, the water streamed down the steep sides of Christie Pits and pooled on the diamonds. Once the diamonds were soaked, they weren't playable. Not until the puddles were dried up by the sun or by the coaches and umpires with rakes and brooms.

But neither of those things could happen until the rain stopped. Looking out his window, Miguel could see that the rain wasn't going to end anytime soon.

Miguel ignored the painful feeling deep in his guts that he had woken up with again. The bad weather seemed to make it worse. He wouldn't be able to play baseball. And that made the day seem hopeless. Baseball always took his mind off his problems. Without it, what did he have except work and worry?

MUDBALL!

A buzz on Miguel's nightstand caught his attention. Another buzz, and he picked up the cell phone to look at messages, one after another. He scanned the goofy Snapchat photos of his friends making silly faces. He smiled. The messages all said the same thing: MUDBALL!

The Blues were sending out the signal for a game of Mudball down at the Pits. That changed everything. Miguel put on his rattiest sweatpants and t-shirt. He clambered downstairs, bringing the phone with him.

"Can you take Claudia today?" Miguel's mother threw a damper on an already damp day.

"Today? It's the weekend!" Miguel said. He handed her the cell phone. "I was going to go play Mudball down at the Pits."

"I'm sorry, Miguel," said his mother. "I was offered an extra shift this weekend. I have to take it."

Miguel knew better than to argue with his mother.

"It'll be fun, Miguel!" said Claudia. She turned her big eyes up to his. "I'll give you my lollipop!"

She held a sticky, green, half-eaten lollipop out to him. Miguel laughed and leaned forward. He took a nibble of it.

"Keep the rest," he said. "And go put on your boots. We're going to play some Mudball!"

★ ★ ★

Down at the Pits, the Mudball game was already on. At the top of the hill, Miguel and Claudia watched the Blues. They were covered in mud. They rolled crazily down the hill as the rain teemed down.

"Boy, this really is a mud-pit!" said Miguel, looking down the hill. He squatted down next to his sister. "One kid is *it*," he explained. "They're the Mudball. When that kid yells 'Mudball!' everyone on the hill has to freeze. Then, the Mudball rolls down the hill and tries to knock each person down. The last one left standing gets to be the Mudball next."

"Hey, everyone!" He greeted his teammates as he led his sister carefully down the slippery hill. "Claudia is going to play too!"

Jock and Sebastian were lying in a tangled, muddy heap. But they managed to wave to Claudia.

"No one had better hurt my sister, okay?" said Miguel. He looked pointedly at Sebastian. "Even by accident! Be careful!"

"I'll protect her!" said Sebastian.

"Just don't get in my way!" said Claudia, her fists on her hips.

Jock laughed and held up his hands. "I definitely won't!" he said.

"MUUUUUUUDBALL!" Sebastian yelled long and loud, from the top of the hill. The gang scattered when they heard him. They froze the instant he'd finished saying the word. Claudia stood like a statue next to Miguel.

"Here he comes," she whispered to Miguel, as Sebastian threw himself down the hill toward them.

"You don't have to whisper, Claudia," said Miguel, laughing. "He's supposed to try to get us!"

Claudia kept her feet planted in the mud. But she swerved her body over as Sebastian hurtled down the hill. He passed her and collided into Lin.

"Got you, Lin!" said Sebastian, untangling himself from his teammate.

"Oh, man!" said Lin. "I thought you were going for Miguel and Claudia!"

"Hah, that's what I wanted you to think!" said Sebastian.

Sebastian turned with an evil grin toward Gnash. He made a giant leap in the air, his arms outstretched.

There was nothing Gnash could do to avoid the boy landing on him. "Get off me!" he yelled. "You idiot! Get off!"

But Sebastian already had his eye on his next victim.

"What about *mee-eee*?" Claudia taunted in a sing-song, waving her arms.

Sebastian looked over. "Good idea." He twirled a make-believe mustache like a villain.

"Be careful, Claudia," Miguel warned.

"I can take care of myself!" she said.

Sebastian rolled toward the girl and gently knocked her over. She sank onto her knees, sliding on the steep, muddy hill. She smiled at her brother.

Miguel gave his sister a quick, muddy hug.

It was pouring rain and he had to babysit his sister, but Miguel felt pretty good. Then he saw that he was the only one still standing.

"My turn to be the Mudball!" he shouted, and ran up the hill.

But when Miguel crested the hill he found his mother waiting there. She was soaking wet, with a concerned look on her face.

"Come, Miguel," she said, holding out her hand. "You and Claudia need to come, now."

13 SIGN LANGUAGE

Miguel didn't waste time asking his mother what the problem was. He slipped and slid down the hill and scooped up his sister. He paused just long enough to tell his friends that he needed to leave.

"Hush, Claudia," he said to his sister, who had started to whine.

"But why do we have to go?" she cried. "You were just about to be the Mudball!"

"I know," Miguel replied. "There will be other Mudball games. Don't worry."

"But I wanted to be the Mudball too!" She was crying for real now.

Miguel puffed as he carried her up the slippery hill. "We'll come back another day."

At the top of the hill, their mother took mud-soaked Claudia from Miguel's arms. She spoke to her daughter soothingly in Spanish. She kissed the top of her head.

"So, what's going on?" Miguel asked his mother.

They had wiped off most of the mud with paper towels and were sitting on the bus.

"It's the bakery." She spoke rapidly and quietly in Spanish.

"Our bakery?" said Claudia. "What's wrong?"

"Nothing for you to worry about, kiddo," said Miguel. "Mom, where's the cell phone?" He found it in her bag and handed it to Claudia. "Here. Play a game."

"Is it the gangs?" Miguel asked his mother.

"Yes," she said. "I don't want to talk about it in front of Claudia. But we need to get your father over here — soon."

"How?"

"I don't know. We have to talk to Mr. Raymond again. That's where we're going now. I need you to translate."

Miguel thought of his friends back in the Pits, covered in mud and having a great time. They would probably head to Pits Pita afterward for lunch and a smoothie. But he had to go to a stupid lawyer's office. It wasn't fair.

"The gangs came to the bakery last night. They tried to set the building on fire," Miguel's mother whispered. Her knuckles were white as she gripped her bag. "Your father is safe, but we need to get him out of El Salvador right away."

Miguel grimaced. All thoughts of Mudball were

suddenly erased from his mind. Now he felt guilty for even thinking of having fun while his father was in trouble.

★ ★ ★

"Hey, I just thought of something," said Sebastian the next day. The team was at Christie Pits on Diamond 1, tossing the ball around. They were waiting for Coach Coop to arrive for their game against the Reds.

"What?" asked Lin, as she blew an enormous bubble. It burst and she smacked her gum hard, chewing it back into bubble-making form.

"No school for us on Friday — PA day!"

"That's right," said Gnash. "No school. No grandparents. No homework. A whole long weekend of nothing but baseball."

"Jock, can you bring a deck of cards for the bus?" Tami threw the ball to him in a long rainbow.

"Yeah, if I remember," said Jock. He caught the ball and fired it back to Tami.

"Text yourself a reminder!" said Tami.

"I'm bringing my swimsuit!" said Sebastian, throwing the ball to Miguel. "I checked out the website. Our hotel has a really nice pool!"

"Gee, that's great," said Miguel.

"Oh, geez," said Sebastian. "Sorry. I forgot."

"Stupid idiot," said Lin to Sebastian. "Way to make him feel bad."

"That's okay," said Miguel. He threw the ball back to Sebastian. "I've got stuff to do."

Miguel saw Lin whisper something he couldn't hear to Sebastian.

"It's really okay, guys," said Miguel. "I can't come. So what? No big deal."

But Miguel's face said it was a big deal. It was a big deal that while the whole team got to hang out and have fun for three days, he would be looking after kids and helping his mother figure out legal stuff. It was a big deal that his family never had enough money or spare time for vacations. It was a big deal that he had never stayed in a hotel in his entire life. *And it's a big deal*, thought Miguel, *that my teammates take everything they have for granted.* Sebastian probably had a swimsuit collection, just like his glove collection!

But Miguel had no more time to dwell on his problems, because Coop arrived. He called the players to the outfield for their pre-game warm-up exercises. Together, the team moved in a pack from the third baseline, lunging and jumping up and lunging again.

When that drill was finished, they all turned toward the infield to do side lunges.

"Come on!" said Coach Coop. "Go down as far as you can. And up. And down!"

When they were finished with the lunges, Coop told everyone to get down on all fours.

"Now lift your left knee up," he said. The teammates lifted one leg up to the side, like a puppy about to pee. They moved the leg around in a circle, to loosen up their hip joint. Then they did the same thing with the other leg.

The drills continued for another ten minutes.

"Okay," said Coop. The team was done and on its feet again. "Pitchers over here."

Jock and Miguel were slated to pitch against the Reds. They followed Coop off to the side. Sebastian ran over, too, pulling his mask down over his face. He joined the pitchers in the bullpen.

Miguel stood on the bullpen mound and threw a slow, easy pitch to Sebastian. It was just wide of the plate.

"Hey, Sebastian. Even though it's just bullpen, you've got to frame those," Coop said.

"What's framing?" asked Miguel.

"That's when I make your terrible pitches look like strikes," said Sebastian.

"It's when the catcher moves the ball over really fast when it hits his glove. He makes it look like it caught the edge of the plate," said Coop.

"When really, it was a ball," said Miguel.

"Right," said Coop. "The best catchers can do it really fast and really subtly, so no one even knows it's happening. But it only works if the pitcher and the catcher are working together, as a team. That's why a lot of pitchers insist on working with just one catcher."

Sebastian and I could never team up that way, thought Miguel. They were too different. Sebastian was the kind of kid who got new baseball gloves whenever he wanted. Who went on vacations with his family and slept in hotels.

And Miguel was the kind of kid who worked.

Miguel shook his head to clear it of the depressing thoughts that were starting to cloud his mind.

"Hey, what was wrong with that?" asked Sebastian. "Fastball down the pipe!"

"Oh! Sorry!" said Miguel. He realized that Sebastian thought he was shaking off his sign for the next pitch. That he didn't want to throw the kind of pitch Sebastian was signalling.

"I wasn't shaking off your sign," said Miguel.

"Geez. Then watch it, will you?"

Sebastian squatted down again and held out his glove.

Miguel threw the ball as hard as he could. It slammed into the centre of Sebastian's glove with a satisfying slap.

"That's better," said Sebastian.

"So are we good with the signs?" Sebastian asked Miguel as the two of them walked onto the field to start the first inning.

"Yes, I told you. It was an accident."

"Okay," said Sebastian.

But Miguel could tell that Sebastian didn't trust him. Well, it was mutual.

"Mr. I-Have-Everything," Miguel whispered under his breath, when he was on the mound. He looked at Sebastian. "You have no idea," he said quietly. "No idea about real life."

14 PERFECT PITCH

The Reds' first batter stepped into the box. Miguel looked at Sebastian for the sign.

Fastball. The same pitch Sebastian had called for during the warm-up.

Miguel shook his head. The first batter was a small, short boy named Ethan. He had long, curly hair that flowed out from under his baseball cap nearly to the middle of his back. And he could run. When Ethan rounded the bases, he ran so fast that his hair billowed out behind him. It reminded Miguel of a superhero with some kind of spectacular cape — but he would never admit that out loud.

Miguel was picturing the boy hitting his fastball and then running, like a blur, to score.

Sebastian called for a fastball again. Again, Miguel shook off the sign.

Sebastian stood up and turned to the umpire. The umpire called "Time!" and held up his hands. Sebastian shoved his mask onto the top of his head and slowly walked out to the mound.

"What are you doing?" Sebastian asked Miguel.

Miguel had his glove over his face so he could talk to the catcher without anyone on the other team overhearing.

"Ethan's small," he said. "He's got a small strike zone. I can't hit that."

"Yes, you can," said Sebastian.

"But all we need is a pop-up to get him out," said Miguel. "If I throw him something slow and inside, he'll pop it up. Perfect. That's better than throwing him a fastball."

"But that's not what will happen," said Sebastian. "He'll pull the ball to left field on a slow-and-inside pitch. Don't do it."

"But I told you, I can't hit that tiny strike zone," said Miguel.

"Yes, you can," said Sebastian. "You've been doing it all week in practice. And I'll help you. I'll frame it."

Miguel could see that Sebastian really believed in him.

"Okay," said Miguel.

"Okay?"

"Yes. I'll trust you."

"Okay," said Sebastian, leaving the mound. He stopped and turned back to Miguel. "You got this," he said.

"Play!" cried the umpire.

Ethan stepped into the batter's box. His long, curly hair wafted over his shoulder. He loaded up his bat and looked expectantly at Miguel.

Sebastian flashed the sign for a fastball.

Miguel nodded. He straightened out his front foot so it was pointing toward the batter, just as Jock had taught him. He brought his hands together in front of him, almost like a prayer. He dropped his throwing arm and then drew it back behind him. Loading onto his back foot, he brought his front knee up high. Then he suddenly shifted his weight and brought his arm forward and down, using it like a slingshot to propel the ball toward Ethan.

"Strike!" Miguel pushed his cap up on his head and then brought it down, tighter. He couldn't believe he'd hit his mark. He brought his hands together again.

Sebastian signalled for another fastball. Miguel hesitated. Hit that spot twice in a row? *Not possible*, thought Miguel.

Sebastian gave him an urgent look. He signalled for another fastball.

Miguel nodded reluctantly. He drew his arm back and shot the ball.

This time, he knew, it was going outside. But when Miguel looked at the ball in Sebastian's mitt, it was over the plate.

"Strike!"

Sebastian gave Miguel a nod. Holding his gaze, he signalled fastball again.

Miguel pictured the blur that Ethan would be as he ran to first base — maybe even second. *Hopefully not third*, thought Miguel. He pictured himself throwing wildly, completely missing the plate. He pictured a come-backer off Ethan's bat hitting him right in the head. All of those things seemed possible. His stomach hurt.

Miguel shook his head to get rid of the thoughts crowding his mind. When he saw Sebastian grimace, he realized he'd done it again. He quickly nodded, to show Sebastian that he agreed to throw a fastball.

"Strike THREE!"

Ethan looked in disbelief as the fastball streaked past him into Sebastian's glove.

"Yerrrr out!"

Miguel pitched most of the rest of that game. Sebastian called the shots and framed his pitches. By the end of the fourth inning, Miguel had thrown just fifty-six pitches.

"Fifty-six in four innings. Wow, that's low," said Sebastian, as the Blues were getting ready to bat.

"Thanks," said Miguel. "You really helped me."

"Naw, it was all you," said Sebastian.

"How'd you know I could hit my targets?"

"I've been watching you. You're not a bad pitcher. All you need is a bit more confidence."

Confidence boosted by the last person I would expect, thought Miguel. *Sebastian*. Sebastian, who he always thought was lazy and slow. But now he looked at the catcher, putting his shin pads and face mask in a neat pile on the bench. And he had to admit that the boy seemed different. *More athletic, maybe*, thought Miguel.

"You know, those morning drills seem to be working for you," he said.

"Thanks," said Sebastian. "Here."

He threw Miguel his batting helmet.

Sebastian strode out to the batter's box while Miguel chose a bat. He went into the on-deck circle and watched the pitcher. When the pitcher threw, Miguel swung at the same time Sebastian did.

Swish!

"Strike one!" said the umpire.

A second fastball came in and Sebastian — and Miguel — swung again.

"Strike two!"

Both boys swung on the third pitch. Miguel's bat sliced through the air. Sebastian's bat connected with the ball. There was a loud *smack* and the ball bounced toward the shortstop. The freight train got going, down to first. But this time, Sebastian reached the base before the shortstop's throw. It was the fastest Miguel had ever seen Sebastian run.

It was Miguel's turn. He stepped into the batter's box.

"C'mon, Miguel!" yelled Lin from the dugout.

Miguel loaded up his bat. The first pitch came, a low fastball. It looked like it was floating, just begging to be hit. Miguel brought his bat around and smashed the ball, taking off running almost at the same time. Miguel flew to first and began to round the base toward second.

Then he saw Sebastian. The catcher hadn't yet reached second. Miguel knew there was no way the boy would be able to make it to third and let Miguel grab a double. He thought briefly about overtaking Sebastian. It would mean an automatic out for Sebastian, but it would put Miguel in a position to score. But that wasn't something you did to a teammate. So Miguel twisted his body and lurched back to first. He threw himself onto the base, barely making it before the tag.

"Unbelievable," he muttered.

15 BELLY FLOP

The Blues won the game 5 to 4, thanks to a home run by Jock that brought Sebastian and Miguel home.

"Thank goodness for that homer, eh, Sebastian?" Miguel asked him after the game.

"What do you mean?" asked Sebastian.

"I mean, we needed the runs to win. And . . ."

"What? I'm still too slow to get home myself?"

"I didn't say that . . ."

"But you were thinking it!"

"It's just that . . . well . . . I thought you were getting in such good shape . . ."

"Look, Miguel, I know you've got a lot of stuff going on at home. I know you're this, like, saint and all. But you're still kind of a jerk to me sometimes!"

Sebastian stuffed the rest of his gear in his bag. He angrily dragged it past Miguel and out of the dugout.

"Did you hear that?" Miguel asked Tami.

"Yep," said Tami.

"What a loser," said Miguel.

"Why?"

"You heard what he said!"

"Well, Miguel, you do sort of treat him pretty harsh."

"What?"

"You look at him like he's the slowest guy on Earth. And he's really trying hard. He's been going to the gym. He's even eating healthy stuff now."

"I know!"

"Maybe you should tell your face," laughed Tami. "You always look so serious. Especially when you're talking to Sebastian. Maybe you could lighten up on him a little?"

Tami's words just made Miguel angrier. No one understood how much pressure he was under. Miguel put a hand on his stomach and pressed his fist into it.

"Miguel! Miguel!"

Claudia came running into the dugout. She threw her arms around Miguel's knees. "You played great, Miguel!" she said, her face shining.

As he looked down at his sister, Miguel no longer felt any pain in his stomach. He kissed her head. "Thanks, Claudia! Where's Mom?"

Claudia took Miguel's hand and led him to where their mother was waiting on the hill. She shook out her blanket and brushed some grass off her knees. She smiled when she saw Miguel.

"Good game!" she said. "We only played soccer

back home, so I don't know much about baseball. But you looked pretty good to me."

Miguel smiled. The three trudged up the hill, Claudia trying to help lift Miguel's heavy baseball bag. At the top, the Blues were gathered. They were talking about the trip they were about to take.

"Hey, what time does your dad want to leave?" Gnash asked Sebastian.

"I think you need to be at our house by 7:15," said Sebastian.

"In the morning?" groaned Gnash.

Tami laughed and took a huge bite of her peanut butter and banana sandwich. "*Mphmf*, if, *mblbbph*, you," she said, still chewing.

"Tami! Swallow first!" said Jock.

Tami gulped her bite down. "If you don't get to Sebastian's house on time, his dad will probably just leave without you!"

"Don't worry. I'll be on time," said Gnash, grinding his teeth. "Gramma will wake me up if I don't hear my alarm. That woman never sleeps! Except when we're watching a movie."

"I love your grandmother," said Raj. "She's so nice!"

"Yeah," said Tami, "And she makes delicious linguini!"

"Hey, Miguel! Are you sure you can't come with us on the trip?" asked Jock. "It's going to be amazing."

"No, I can't," said Miguel. He glanced back at his mother. He didn't want her to hear what his teammates were talking about. He knew she already felt bad that she couldn't let him go. "But you guys go and have a great time. Win it, eh?"

"We will!" said Raj.

Miguel slapped him a high-five and then bent down and picked up Claudia. "Come on," he said to her, giving her a little squeeze.

He walked with Claudia to the bus stop. But he realized his mother wasn't with them. He saw her talking to Sebastian and the other Blues. He watched as she pulled something in silver foil from her purse and handed it to the catcher.

"What was that about?" Miguel asked his mother, when they were on the bus.

"Nothing," she said pleasantly. "Just wishing them a good trip. I gave them some pupusas."

As the bus drove away, Miguel could hear his teammates. They were laughing and talking about their plans for the Ottawa tournament.

★ ★ ★

Over the next three days, Miguel stayed busy with work. He tried to keep his mind off the fact that his friends were all in Ottawa, playing baseball and having fun. But it wasn't easy. He got a steady stream of texts from his teammates. He guessed that things weren't going well for the Blues.

Jock texted:

We got mercied by the Ottawa Otters. Four errors!

Followed by Gnash:

Raj pitched 💩 2day. 2 bad U arnt here.

Tami sent Miguel a series of pictures of her meals. Spaghetti and meatballs. Fried chicken. A hamburger.

Cannonball!

The text from Sebastian was followed by a shaky video of the boy launching himself stomach-first into the deep end of the hotel pool. He emerged from the water with his hair over his eyes and a pained expression on his face.

Miguel texted back:

Not a cannonball. Belly flop

He added a 😄.

Miguel's mother knocked on his bedroom door.

"Come in," he said.

"Mr. Raymond is on the phone," she said. "Can you come talk to him?"

Miguel nodded. "I don't think the Blues are going to the finals," he said.

"No?"

"Sounds like they will be lucky to make the quarter-finals on Saturday night."

"Oh dear."

"Yeah. Gnash said he wished I could be there."

Miguel's mother sat on the edge of his bed. She put a hand on his knee. "So do I," she said. "Come — let's find out what Mr. Raymond wants."

16 FEET FIRST

Miguel could see the relief on his mother's face. He had almost forgotten how her face looked when she wasn't worried. Smoother and softer. The lawyer had told them the papers went through. It wouldn't be long before Miguel's father could come to Canada.

"In fact, if you can give me a cheque for the airfare, we can probably get that booked," said Mr. Raymond.

Miguel repeated in Spanish what the lawyer had said.

"How much will that cost?" Miguel's mom asked.

"Mom, this is good news. He's saying we can book the flight! We're finally going to have Dad home!"

"But, Miguel, I don't have the money for the airfare yet," said his mother. "I didn't know we would need it so soon."

Miguel saw the worry flood back onto his mother's face.

"We'll just have to get it," said Miguel. "Somehow."

He smiled at his mother. But inside, his guts twisted.

They were barely paying their lawyer's bills, never mind things like power and water and rent. They were behind in paying the league for their baseball fees, too, and that was with a special discount. How were they going to come up with money for a plane ticket?

★ ★ ★

"Miguel, watch me!" shouted Julian. "Watch me!"

It was a few days after the Blues had returned from Ottawa. Miguel was pushing Claudia on the swing. At the same time, he had an eye on two other kids he was babysitting. Since learning that his family would need to pay for a plane ticket, Miguel had doubled up on his babysitting. He wanted to do everything he could to help.

"That's great, Julian," Miguel shouted to the boy, who was spinning around with his arms out. Julian fell down, laughing.

Miguel smiled. "Claudia, I have to go over and get Julian," he told his sister.

After he had picked up Julian and set him on his feet, Miguel loped over to the slide. Little Heather was about to go down head-first.

"Nope," said Miguel. He picked her up and set her on her bottom at the top of the slide. "We go feet-first. Head-first is dangerous."

"But it's fun!" Heather protested.

"Look, I don't get paid unless you're alive at the end of the day," said Miguel with a laugh. "Now how do we go down a slide?"

"*Feeeet. Firrrrrst.*" Heather frowned. "The boring way!"

"Right!" said Miguel. He spun around just in time to catch Claudia trying to climb out of her swing seat. She was stuck, half in and half out. She had one leg in the hole and one in mid-air.

"I've got you!" said Miguel. He grabbed hold of his sister and untangled her from the swing.

As soon as Miguel set her down, Claudia skipped away to the sand pit to play with Julian and Heather.

"What are you doing?" It was Sebastian, coming up the path behind Miguel. Sebastian was wearing sweatpants and a blue t-shirt so soaked with sweat it looked black.

"I'm babysitting. What are *you* doing?"

"I'm stepping up my routine," said Sebastian. "Jogging."

"Hey, that's grea —" Miguel suddenly broke off and sped over to the slide. He caught Heather just as she was about to fly off the end. He rolled his eyes at Sebastian. "I'm watching three of them at once."

"That's three kids too many, if you ask me," said Sebastian.

"Come and help me at the swings," said Miguel. "I hate pushing the kids on the swings. It's so boring."

"I thought you liked this stuff."

"Not really. I'd way rather be playing baseball."

"Yeah. I keep forgetting that you weren't at the tournament," said Sebastian. "It was so fun."

"So I heard," said Miguel.

The boys pushed Claudia and Julian on the swings. All the while, Miguel kept glancing over at Heather digging in the sandpit.

"I just found out that my dad can come to Canada," said Miguel.

"That's great!" said Sebastian. "You've been waiting a long time."

"Yeah. But we also found out that we have to buy a plane ticket first."

"So?"

"So, do you know what it costs to fly from El Salvador to Canada?"

"No idea. A lot?"

"A lot." Sebastian didn't seem to know what to say to that.

"Hey, what about a loan?" said Sebastian.

"Sure," said Miguel. "You want to lend me four hundred bucks?"

Sebastian whistled. "That much, eh?"

"More, actually. Like, four-eighty."

The boys gave the swings another push.

"Maybe my parents could," said Sebastian.

"Could what?" asked Miguel.

"Lend your mom the money."

"My parents would never take someone's money."

"Why not?" Sebastian seemed truly surprised by Miguel's reaction.

"Maybe you've never had to ask someone for charity," said Miguel slowly.

"Charity? This wouldn't be charity! It would be a loan," said Sebastian. "A loan to my favourite teammate."

Miguel felt his face getting red. *Sebastian has no idea of the situation*, he thought. Nearly five hundred dollars? It was an unbelievable sum of money. More than he would make in a year babysitting. That anyone — even someone as rich as Sebastian's parents — would have money like that to spare for someone they barely knew. It was unthinkable. Anyway, he knew his mother would never accept money from anyone — and neither would his father.

"I'll let you know tonight. I'll text you," said Sebastian.

Miguel was moved by his friend's offer to help, even if it was impossible.

"Watch this," said Sebastian. He grabbed Claudia's swing by the sides. He ran forward and ducked down, going right under. He gave a mighty shove up on the swing as he ran. The swing went up high. Claudia, giggling, made a tremendous arc in the air.

"Oh geez," said Miguel. "Now they're all going to want me to do that!"

"Ha! That was the idea," said Sebastian.

"Under-duck! Under-duck!" cried Julian, seeing Claudia's exciting swing.

"Well, see you," said Sebastian, as he walked away. "I have to finish my run!"

"Under-duck!" cried Heather.

Suddenly, Sebastian stopped. He turned to look back at Miguel.

"Hey, I'll see you tonight!" he called.

"What? Where?" asked Miguel, confused.

"At your house! You know . . ." Suddenly, the catcher put his hands over his mouth. He turned and jogged away.

17 FELIX CRUMPLES

Miguel had no idea what Sebastian was talking about. But he didn't have time to think about it. The kids kept him busy until late afternoon. By the time he'd walked Julian and Heather home, it was nearly time for dinner.

As he came up the path with Claudia to their front door, he was surprised to hear voices — lots of them. Then he thought about what Sebastian had said in the park.

Miguel and Claudia stepped into their seemingly empty living room. Suddenly, it was filled with his teammates. They popped out from behind the furniture. "SURPRISE!"

A colourful plastic banner stretched along the wall over the couch: "Feliz Cumpleaños."

Miguel turned to his mother, who was coming out of the kitchen. She wiped her hands on a dishtowel. "But my birthday isn't for another week," he said.

She smiled. "I know, but it's close enough. And the

timing worked out for the team. I talked to Sebastian after the game the other day. He arranged for everyone to come here." She gave her son a peck on the cheek.

The teammates swarmed Miguel. They patted him on the back and wished him a happy birthday. Miguel looked around to find Sebastian, but couldn't spot him.

Claudia jumped up and down. "Let's do the presents!" she cried.

Miguel saw a pile of gifts on the dining room table. He let himself be led over to a chair.

Tami put a red envelope into his hands. Smiling, Miguel ripped it open. "Custom sandwiches," he read, flipping through a handful of hand-drawn coupons.

"I'll make you any kind of sandwich you want," said Tami. "I'll even wrap it up and bring it to school for you. Tuna. Cheese. Meatloaf. Whatever you want!"

Gnash handed him a small box. Miguel ripped off the wrapping paper to reveal . . . "Chewing gum! Shredded like big-league chew. And it's my favourite flavour — grape!"

"Now mine!" said Claudia. She handed him a homemade card. On the front was a drawing of a baseball team.

"Did you draw this?" Miguel asked his sister.

"Yes!" said Claudia. She pointed to the crayon figures. "That's you, pitching. And that's Jock. And that's Tami and there's Gnash and Lin and Raj and . . ."

"Am I in there?" said a familiar voice. Sebastian

strode into the living room. He was holding a large gift-wrapped box.

"Sebastian!" said Claudia. She ran over to the boy and gave him a hug. "You're right here," she said pointing to the picture.

Inside the card was Claudia's gift. "I will sing you a song," it read.

Claudia ran out of the room. When she came back, she was lugging a guitar, which she handed to Miguel.

"Here," she said. "You play and I'll sing."

Miguel laughed and rested the guitar on his knee. He strummed.

"I didn't know you played guitar!" said Jock.

"In El Salvador everyone plays guitar. It's practically our national pastime," said Miguel.

Claudia began to sing.

Arrurru, mi niño
Cabeza de ayote,
Si no te dormís
Te come el coyote

"That's beautiful," said Tami, when the song ended.

"Thank you," said Claudia. She looked at her brother and smiled.

"It is a very popular lullaby," said Miguel. He and Claudia laughed.

"Yes, it means go to sleep or a coyote will eat you!" said Claudia happily.

"It really doesn't translate well," explained Miguel. The teammates laughed.

"My gift next," said Sebastian, handing Miguel the box. "It's not new, but I hope you like it. I went all the way home to get it."

Miguel pulled something large and heavy, wrapped in tissue paper, out of the box.

"Sebastian, it's your new infield glove!"

"Well you said you liked it. And I saw that the laces on yours were kind of fraying. Plus, you said yourself, there was nothing wrong with my old glove. Anyway, I barely use it. I mostly use my catcher's mitt. Do you like it?"

Miguel stood up and walked over to Sebastian. He hugged the catcher.

"Thank you," he choked. "But I can't accept it!"

"Yes you can, and you will," said Sebastian.

"No, really," said Miguel. He whispered urgently to his friend. "It's so expensive and . . ."

"Look, is your other glove a mess?"

"Yes, but —"

"And is it hard for you to catch long-balls with it?"

"Yes, but —"

"I don't know about you, but I'd like to win some more games this season. And if you go dropping all the balls . . . you won't be much good to us, will you?

This isn't just for you. It's for the team."

Miguel laughed. "Okay, I give in," he said.

"Happy birthday, my friend. And to Felix Crumples, whoever he is!" Sebastian gestured at the birthday banner.

Miguel laughed.

The smell of something delicious suddenly captured everyone's attention. Miguel saw that his mother had set out plates of food. There were tamales and fried plantains and pupusas. There was a delicious cabbage salad and a big bowl of soup loaded with beef and vegetables.

"Come on, kids," Miguel's mother said. "Eat up!"

Tami was the first to reach the table. "Look at these tamales!" she exclaimed.

After the meal, Miguel's mother served squares of cake topped with whipped cream, strawberries and almonds.

Miguel stood up. He cleared his throat.

"I want to thank you," he said. He had one arm around his mother and the other around Claudia. "It was not easy for us when we moved here three years ago. But having friends like you, it makes me feel . . ."

Miguel saw that Sebastian and Jock had tears in their eyes.

"I'm sorry," said Miguel. "I'm terrible at speeches. But I have good news. We just found out that our father will soon be allowed to come to Canada!"

"But I thought —" said Sebastian.

"He's coming, Sebastian. We're not exactly sure how we can make it happen. But nothing is going to stop him from joining us."

"But —"

"No buts, Sebastian," Miguel cut him off again. "This is a happy day."

"But I thought he couldn't come because you need money for the plane ticket!" Sebastian blurted out before Miguel could stop him.

"What's that?" asked Gnash.

"They don't have enough money for the plane ticket," said Sebastian, loudly.

"Sebastian!" said Jock. "They might not want everyone to know that!"

"I tried to ask my parents for a loan, but they said they couldn't," said Sebastian. "I've been feeling really bad about it. I'm so sorry, Miguel."

"That's okay," said Miguel. "I wouldn't have been able to take your parents' money, anyway."

Suddenly, he thought about his sister. He looked down at her.

Claudia's eyes were brimming with tears. "Does this mean Daddy can't come to Canada?" she asked.

"Of course not," said Miguel. "It just means it might take a little bit longer."

Claudia started crying for real. Tears flowed down her face as she became more and more upset. Miguel picked her up and hugged her, but she squirmed out of his grasp.

"But he's not safe!" said Claudia, through her tears. "He might get hurt! He needs to come here now!"

"Why?" asked Gnash.

Briefly, Miguel explained his father's situation to his teammates.

"Then Claudia's right. We have to bring him over. Now," said Tami.

"For sure," said Jock.

"But how?" asked Gnash. "You just heard Sebastian say they don't have the money for a plane ticket."

"I've got more babysitting jobs lined up," said Miguel. "Don't worry, you guys."

"We have to do something. Think, everyone," said Gnash.

"Miguel, can I speak with you a minute?" Miguel's mother called him into the kitchen.

"I know, I know," began Miguel.

"I like your friends, Miguel. I really do. But you know how your father and I feel about charity. We can't accept it, no matter how kindly it is offered," said Miguel's mother.

"I know," repeated Miguel.

"Please, talk to your friends."

"I will, Mama," said Miguel.

18 BIG PLANS

"Hey, what about a home-run derby?" asked Sebastian as Miguel came back from the kitchen.

"Sebastian, this is no time to think about games. We've got a serious problem to solve," said Tami. She rolled her eyes.

"Why do you always have to be goofing around, Sebastian?" asked Gnash. "This is important."

"No!" said Sebastian. "I mean, we can hold a home-run derby to raise money for Mr. Estrada's plane ticket!"

"You know, guys, that's not totally stupid," said Gnash.

"We could have a best-hitter competition. Everyone could pay five bucks to hit," said Jock. "The longest hit wins a prize or something."

"And a longest-throw contest," said Tami. "And a sprinting competition. The fastest time around the bases wins."

"There could be a box for donations," said Jock.

"We could hold an exhibition game with those

rich Parkhill Pirates!" said Gnash. "They have tons of money! We'll take their parents' money — and then totally beat them on the field!"

"I kind of like that idea," said Jock.

"My mom's company makes toys. I'm sure I could get them to donate some prizes," said Lin. "Maybe stuffed animals or baseballs or something."

"And Mommy can sell pupusas and tamales and empanadas," said Claudia.

"Guys!" said Miguel. "Hey, guys!" He held up his hands.

"What?" asked Tami. She had gone back for more food. Now she was shovelling soup into her mouth.

"Stop! Please, stop. We can't do this," said Miguel.

"What? Why not?" asked Sebastian.

"I know you mean well. But this just isn't what our family does."

"What, you mean accept payback for everything you've done for us?" asked Jock.

"What do you mean?" asked Miguel.

"Remember last year, when those stupid Pirates were on my case?"

"Of course," said Miguel.

"You were one of the first ones to help me," said Jock. "You even yelled at Stretch!"

"And you practically wrote my history essay last term," said Gnash.

"Yeah, and my belly's been full of your mom's pupusas all month," said Tami. "And sopa and tres leches cake and . . ."

"This isn't charity," said Gnash. "Believe me, I'm the last one who would be giving stuff away!"

"This is just what a team does," said Jock.

"Besides, it wouldn't be only for you," said Tami.

"It wouldn't?" asked Miguel. He was so distracted, he didn't hear his mother come into the room.

"No! It would also be to let people know what's happening in El Salvador."

"How much do you think we could raise?" asked Sebastian.

"I bet we could raise enough to pay for the ticket. And to put some in a fund for other families in the neighbourhood," said Jock. "There's a group that helps newcomers."

Miguel's mother put her arm around his shoulders and gave him a squeeze. "Miguel, if it would help other families . . ." she said. Miguel looked hopefully at her, and she nodded.

Soon the excited Blues were all talking over one another with ideas and suggestions. It was a long time before anyone noticed the music coming from the corner of the room.

"Hey, shush, you guys!" said Tami. "*Sssssssh!* Listen!" She pointed to the corner where Miguel sat, strumming his guitar.

Miguel began to sing in Spanish. His voice surrounded his teammates like a warm blanket. It was a song none of them knew, but they listened, entranced.

"He sounds amazing," said Sebastian, poking Tami in the arm.

"*Sssssssh!*" Tami shushed him.

Miguel finished his song and put down his guitar. There was silence in the room as the music settled.

And then, all Miguel's friends burst into applause.

★ ★ ★

The team had gone home and his mother had put Claudia to bed. Miguel got out the family's laptop to call his father on Skype. He wanted to see his father's face and ask him if they could go ahead with the fundraiser.

The house was quiet. Mr. Estrada's gentle face and warm eyes peered out of the glow of the screen. Miguel's mother came into the room and quietly handed her son a mug of steaming, milky tea. She leaned over so her husband could see her face. She smiled at him.

Miguel told his father about the party. And having to babysit three kids at once.

"And Claudia got stuck!" he said.

"Stuck? Where?" asked his father. His eyes crinkled with laughter.

"In the swing! I had to dive over to catch her!"

Miguel heard a loud banging noise coming from another part of his father's house. It sounded like someone knocking hard on his father's front door.

"What's that?" Miguel asked.

His father turned to look behind him. "I have to go," he said.

"Why, Dad? What's going on?"

"Nothing for you to worry about," his father said. "Really. I'll be fine. This is just a normal part of life in this neighbourhood now. I will see you soon, in person! Just look after your sister for me. And listen to your mother! I love you."

The screen went black as his father signed off. Slowly, Miguel pulled the screen down and clicked the laptop shut.

He needed to get his father out of El Salvador. He thought about what his teammates had said. How accepting help was all just part of being on a team. About how he, too, gave to his teammates. And about how the fund could help other families.

Fighting a wave of pain building in his stomach, he knew he needed to do something — right now. He found a lined notepad and a pen and wrote: *FUNDRAISER.*

Underneath, he wrote the numbers 1 to 10. He started to list the things he needed to do to get ready.

1) Ask Mr. Raymond: Date dad can leave
2) Christie Pits park permit
3) Call Pirates for exhibition game

Soon, Miguel realized how many little things had to get done. Arrange hitting contest. Get signs for throwing contest. Get tickets. Prizes. Microphone for announcements. Advertise the event. Get sponsors. Write a Facebook post. Ask Ben if he would volunteer to ump.

His list went on and on. How could Miguel possibly do all of it? And he still had his babysitting jobs taking up his time.

A sharp knock took his attention away from the list. Miguel padded to the front door, not wanting his sister and mother to be disturbed by the noise. He was surprised at who he found on his front step.

"Hi! Sorry to disturb you this late. But I forgot those pupusas your mom packed for me," said Sebastian. "I was nearly all the way home when I remembered. I asked my dad to turn the car around and come right back."

"Come in," said Miguel. "They're in a bag on the counter. I'll get it."

"Hey, what's this?" asked Sebastian. He picked up Miguel's list. Sebastian scanned the long string of items and then whistled. "Geez," he said.

"Yeah," said Miguel.

"So you're thinking we can do this thing?"

"Well, I didn't get a chance to ask my dad. But since it'll raise money for other people too, I think he'll go for it."

"Good! But look at this list! I had no idea it would be this much work."

Miguel chuckled. "You never do, Sebastian!"

"Don't worry. I'll call a team meeting. We'll meet at lunch tomorrow. And we'll . . . we'll delegate!"

"Delegate?" asked Miguel. "What do you mean?"

"Well, when my mom runs a big charity event, she gets everyone to do stuff. Like, Lin can be in charge of the prizes. And Gnash can get us his grandfather's microphone, and maybe do online publicity. Raj can call about the permits — he's good at dealing with adults. Jock can set up the throwing contest. And I'm sure Tami will help your mom with the bake sale. As long as your mom can keep her from eating all the profits!"

Miguel stared at Sebastian. Could he possibly accept all that help from his teammates? How could he ask everyone to do so much work?

All of a sudden, it was just too much. Accepting charity. Worrying about his father. The surprise birthday party. Sebastian's amazing gift. He lurched forward and clutched Sebastian in a big bear hug.

And he let his tears flow.

19 DERBY DAY

People crowded into the Pits under the bright sun. Miguel watched them come out of the subway station and line up to buy tickets for the competitions. He saw them flock to the bake table. They bought cupcakes and licked the icing that the sun melted down the sides.

Miguel and the Blues helped with the throwing competition on Diamond 2 and the hitting contest on Diamond 1. Miguel watched as adults dropped money in the donation box, which slowly grew fuller.

"Some people are here to compete," said Jock. "Some of them live near the Pits, or want to support new Canadians. But everyone's here for your mother's delicious food!"

Just after lunch, Miguel heard a low rumble at the west side of the park. He saw a convoy of black SUVs pull into the parking lot above Diamond 2. He watched the Parkhill Pirates get out of the SUVs and stream down into the ballpark. Their white uniforms glowed in the sun as they began warming up.

He watched as the Pirates' parents and siblings made their way to the tables, where they bought tickets and food and made generous donations. He even saw Stretch, the Pirate who had treated Jock with such prejudice and anger, sample the pupusas and drop some of his allowance money in the donation box.

"Pirate money," joked Sebastian. "That's okay — we'll take money off those guys any time!"

"This is going really well, isn't it?" asked Miguel, as they watched the batters line up to compete. Sebastian had a fistful of tickets he had collected from the kids in the line-up, each one worth a dollar.

"Here, I'll take those over to the ticket box for you," Miguel told Sebastian. He hardly knew how to thank his teammates. He never dreamed that people even knew — much less cared — about the struggles of newcomers to Canada.

And then, he knew what he had to do. It was outside his comfort zone, but he also knew someone who would help him.

"Sebastian," said Miguel. "I need to thank everyone. But I'm not really comfortable speaking to crowds . . ."

"Here, let me," said Sebastian. He grabbed the wireless microphone.

"EXCUSE ME!" he said. He tapped the mic and it squealed.

The crowd turned toward the sound.

"A-HEM! EXCUSE ME!" he said, even louder. Another squeal from the microphone.

Few could resist Sebastian's warm, goofy grin as he stood waiting until the crowd hushed.

"I want to thank everyone for coming out today," he said. "As you know, we are in the final stages of bringing someone very special into this community. Jose Estrada is the father of one of our own Blues players. We want to welcome him to Canada and reunite him with his family."

The crowd clapped.

"We also want to thank our city councillors, Beau Maverick and Spike Leighton, for helping to arrange the permits for today's event." Miguel smiled over at two men standing near the bake table. They had also helped smooth out the paperwork for his family more than once.

The crowd applauded again. Sebastian turned to put the microphone back on the table, but Miguel took it from him.

If Sebastian can try to change, thought Miguel, *I can try too*. He swallowed.

"Thanks, Sebastian," he said tentatively into the microphone. He cleared his throat. "THANK YOU, SEBASTIAN," he said, more clearly.

The crowd looked expectantly at Miguel.

"I would like to thank my teammates."

There was whooping and hollering from the Blues.

"And in particular, Sebastian. He's our catcher."

Sebastian's face turned red. He took a deep, dramatic bow, to the delight of the audience.

"You may think we are unlikely friends." Miguel heard chuckles from the crowd. "And you'd be right. But I have come to realize some things about Sebastian. Not only is he a talented ball player. But his heart is as big as anyone's I have ever known. I will never forget what he has done for our family and other families like ours in this community. And I will never forget what you all have done. Thank you. Oh, and one last thing —" Miguel turned to look at Coach Coop. "GO BLUES!"

The crowd burst into what sounded to Miguel like thunderous applause. Sebastian turned and slapped him on the back. Miguel was happy. Sebastian could be silly and clumsy and irresponsible. But Miguel now knew that those things were nothing compared to his many good qualities.

"I've got another surprise for you, my friend," Sebastian said to Miguel.

"What?"

"I know you have to babysit tomorrow. The surprise is that I'm going to babysit for you. I want you to have a day off. You can do whatever you want. Have fun! I'll take care of the kids."

He looked at Miguel, who wasn't smiling. "Isn't that awesome?" asked Sebastian, a little less forcefully.

"Uh," said Miguel. "Um . . ."

"It'll be great! I'll take them to the park. They can use the pizza oven. And we'll go horseback riding. And scuba diving in the lake. I might even take them zip-lining, if we have time, after we go on the trampoline."

"Sebastian, they're four years old."

"Okay. Well, maybe not zip-lining, then."

"How about you come along and just help me babysit," said Miguel. "We'll push them on the swings."

Miguel smiled at his friend.

"Okay, whatever you want." Sebastian scratched his head.

"Boy, ya try to help some people," Miguel heard him mutter.

20 HOME TEAM

Miguel was ready for the big exhibition game.

The umpires called for the coaches and team reps to meet at home plate. They would go over the ground rules and do the coin toss.

"Hey, Miguel!" called Coach Coop.

Miguel ran out of the dugout to join his coach.

"You do the toss," said Coop. He handed Miguel a large coin.

Miguel felt his hand shake as he took the coin. He didn't want to mess up.

He looked around. He saw his mother helping a line of customers at the bake table. He saw Sebastian, in the dugout, pulling on his catcher's gear. And he saw the overflowing donation bin, guarded by Tami's older sister, Pamela. She was eating a big blue cupcake, and keeping a careful eye on the money.

Like sister, like sister, thought Miguel, happily.

"Toss the coin," said Coop.

Miguel balanced the coin on his thumb and flicked it up into the air. The coin spun once, twice, three times.

"Heads!" said Coop, while the coin was in the air.

Miguel caught the coin in his right hand and, in the same motion, flipped it onto the back of his left hand. He peeled his right hand up a bit. The coin had landed heads up.

Miguel looked at Coop.

"Home!" said Miguel.

"Yep, we're home," said Coop, looking fondly at the boy. The two jogged to the dugout.

★ ★ ★

Jock pitched the first three innings, with Miguel playing first base. For once, it had been a rough start for Jock, who had walked five Pirates. And most of the other Pirates were hitting off him. But the Blues' defence had held their own. The Blues' shortstop, Gnash, had managed to tag the Pirates runner out to end the last half-inning.

By the middle of the fourth inning, the game was tied 3–3. Two Blues had struck out.

Tami "took" the first pitch of the fourth inning, letting the ball whiz by her ankles without swinging at it.

"Ball," said Ben, the umpire.

Tami swung at the second pitch, connecting with the ball for a line drive up the middle. The Pirates' shortstop fielded the ball off the ground. But then he panicked, seeing Tami speeding toward first. He threw wildly. The ball went over the head of the Pirates' first baseman. Tami ran to second and the crowd in the Pits cheered.

Jock was up next. Miguel was about to enter the on-deck circle when Sebastian caught his arm.

"Wait," he said, urgently. "I have a feeling they're up to something."

"Aren't they always?" asked Miguel.

"Yeah, but I've been watching their coach. He's plotting."

"Maybe. But what can I do about it?"

"I'm not sure. Stay smart out there," said Sebastian. "There are two out. We only need one run to pull ahead. Don't get caught."

"Batter!" the ump called, impatiently.

"If I figure out what's going on, I'll try to let you know," said Sebastian.

Miguel couldn't imagine what Sebastian could possibly learn about the other team's tactics. But he decided to trust Sebastian's baseball instincts. He nodded at Sebastian.

From the on-deck circle, Miguel could see Sebastian watching the Pirates like a hawk. Miguel turned away to watch the pitcher. Every time Jock swung his bat, Miguel swung too. Miguel thought he had the pitcher's timing down.

"Ohhhhhhhh!" The crowd cried out as a ball hit Jock squarely on the leg.

"Way to wear it!" shouted Sebastian.

Jock walked awkwardly to first base, clearly trying not to limp or rub his leg. When he reached first, Miguel stepped into the batter's box.

Hitting Jock appeared to have shaken the pitcher. His first pitch was right down the centre of the plate. Miguel assumed it was meant to be a fastball. It was anything but. Miguel swung hard and hit the ball on his bat's sweet spot. He ran as fast as he could for first. Jock took off for second and made it to third by the time the Pirates managed to get control of the ball and send it to first. Miguel had already touched the base and was skidding to a stop a few feet past it.

"Safe!" said the umpire, spreading his arms wide.

Tami had crossed the plate. That put the Blues one run ahead with two out.

Coop gave Miguel the "steal" sign. Miguel waited for his chance. When the Pirates' first pitch was a high ball, he sped to second.

The field umpire swept his arms wide. Safe.

"Ball one," said Ben.

Jock was at third. Miguel was on second and no one was on first. There were two out.

Sebastian came up to bat. Miguel heard one of the Pirates' outfielders yell, "Muscles!"

The outfielders moved back. The infielders moved onto the grass.

Sebastian rolled his eyes and stepped out of the batter's box. He caught Miguel's eye and pointed to the Pirates' coach. He was holding up four fingers.

"That means intentional walk," Miguel muttered.

The Pirates saw something in Sebastian that Miguel hadn't noticed. Sebastian had muscles. He looked fit. He looked like a big hitter. So they were going to walk him on purpose rather than let him hit it out of the park.

Walking him would load the bases. But with two out, a play at any base would end the inning.

The Pirates' catcher hopped a step to his right, well away from the plate. He held his glove out in front of him and the pitcher lobbed the ball into it.

"Ball," said the umpire.

The catcher returned to his spot behind the plate.

The pitcher went into a loose wind-up. Again, the catcher hopped to the side and caught the ball over the dirt.

"Ball two," said the umpire.

Sebastian watched the proceedings with a smile on his face. Being walked in this league was a sign that you were a real athlete, and everyone knew it. Sebastian wore it like a badge of pride.

"Ball three!"

There was muttering from the bleachers as some parents began to catch on to what was happening. Coop gave Sebastian a thumbs-up sign, which Sebastian tried to ignore. However, it was clear the boy was enjoying his moment.

"Ball four, take your base," said Ben. The umpire stretched out one arm to usher Sebastian to first. The parents on the Blues' side of the line, along with some of the kids at the bake table, clapped as he walked to first base.

It was Gnash's turn to bat. He looked at the loaded bases. For the first time since Miguel had known him, Gnash looked nervous in the batter's box. But he stepped in and loaded up his bat.

Suddenly . . .

"Time!" yelled the umpire.

The Pirates' coach had stopped the play. He headed out to the mound.

Miguel watched as the tall coach talked to his pitcher. The pitcher nervously jostled the baseball from one hand to the other. The coach put his hand on the boy's shoulder.

Then Miguel saw Sebastian leave his base and run to join him at second.

"They're going to try to pick you off," whispered Sebastian.

21 SAFE AT HOME

"Stay awake out there, Miguel. And watch the pitcher. Don't get picked off," said Sebastian.

"How do you know what they're planning?" asked Miguel.

"Look, I only have a second! Just *trust* me," said Sebastian.

Sebastian turned and waved to Jock. Sebastian lifted one leg and twisted it around. Then he pretended to throw. The whole imaginary scene was over in a second. But it was clear that Sebastian was warning Jock about a pickoff too.

Jock nodded.

The Pirates' coach left the mound.

After Sebastian's warning, Miguel kept his eyes on the pitcher. He didn't expect the boy to look over at him. Most pitchers were smart enough not to do that, because it would make it obvious they were going to try a pickoff.

Miguel was watching for movement in the

pitcher's back foot. If the boy was going to throw a normal pitch, that leg would be planted firmly on the ground. But for a pickoff, he'd probably make a little jump-move. And for that, he'd first have to raise his back heel. That would let him pivot off the rubber and throw.

Pickoffs at second were tricky. Right-handed pitchers had to twist all the way around and look for the person on base. That is, assuming there was some-one there to throw to. They also had to make sure they didn't get called on a balk.

"Play!" yelled the umpire.

The pitcher twisted his front foot into the dirt. He lifted his hands and put them together in front of him.

And then, Miguel saw his back heel come up.

Miguel dove back to second base. The pitcher pivoted. Miguel heard the Pirates' second baseman sprint to the base. Miguel's hands reached the base in a cloud of dust, just as the pitcher launched the ball.

"Safe!"

Miguel was well safe, thanks to Sebastian's warning.

He didn't know how Sebastian had read the pitch-er's mind. He stood up and put one foot on the base. He brushed the dust off his pants. Over at first base, Sebastian gave him a smile and a thumbs-up.

"Sebastian," Miguel said softly, "You are one unusual kid."

CRACK!

Gnash connected with the ball. It went soaring out to centre field. The crowd started yelling. Miguel watched Coop windmill him around third base toward home.

Behind him, he heard a voice he knew.

"Hey, slow poke! Go faster, eh?"

It was Sebastian. He was closing in on him. Miguel smiled and put on a burst of speed. Sebastian couldn't quite catch up. But Miguel was surprised at how close they were as they headed down the line to the plate.

Miguel had to find a way to get to the plate before the catcher did, or they would both be out. He shut his eyes and threw himself feet-first at home plate. He felt his heels carve into the dirt, and then felt his foot catch on the plate.

"Safe!"

Miguel got to his feet, and then . . . *wham!* Sebastian body-slammed him in a bear hug that lifted him off the ground. The entire team poured out of the dugout and began high-fiving as Gnash made it all the way to third base.

His three-run triple had made the Blues unstoppable. The game ended, four innings later, 9–3 for the home team.

In the dugout after the game, Miguel was finally able to ask Sebastian the question on his mind.

"How'd you know the pitcher was going to try to pick me off?" Miguel asked his sweaty teammate.

"Simple. It was a strange time for the coach to call a time out. So I knew it wasn't just a pep talk. Plus, I'd seen the coaches yammering together the whole inning. I told you they were planning something."

"You're like a baseball mind-reader," said Miguel, chuckling.

"Naw. It's just smart play," said Sebastian.

"Einstein!" said Miguel, patting his friend on the back.

The boys were interrupted by a ringing sound. Miguel ran over to his baseball bag and took out his mother's cell phone.

"Hello?"

"How is the fundraiser going?" his father asked in Spanish.

"Fantastic!"

"I'm glad to hear it."

"Why? Are things bad there?"

"Not great. But I'm fine right now."

"But you'd like to be getting on a plane."

"Right."

Miguel put the phone on speaker. He walked his father over to the bake table and handed the phone to his mother. She held it up so everyone could hear.

"*Mrhph* . . . it's going . . . gulp . . . really well, Mr. Estrada," said Tami's sister loudly. She held the cash box up to the phone and shook it so he could hear the coins.

"And Jose," said Miguel's mom, "I had the best news today! One of the mothers from the Pirates tried my empanadas. She wants me to cater a party next month!"

"That's great!" Miguel said.

"If that goes well, she said it could lead to other catering jobs."

"We could start the bakery over again, in Canada," said Miguel's father through the phone.

"This makes me almost appreciate the Pirates," said Sebastian. He took a big bite of a cupcake. "Almost!"

Claudia ran up to Sebastian. "Come on!" she said, pulling at his arm.

"I told her I'd play catch with her and Alejandro," said Sebastian. He let himself be dragged away by the little girl.

"Do we trust him with the children?" Miguel's mother asked.

Miguel turned to watch Sebastian and the kids walking toward Diamond 2. Sebastian held each child by the hand. Both children were talking non-stop, vying for the boy's attention. He was listening to them and nodding. Then he stopped and dropped Alejandro's hand. He went down on one knee in front of Claudia.

Miguel resisted the urge to jog over to see what the problem was.

Sebastian reached over and carefully refastened the Velcro on Claudia's shoe. Then he stood up and brushed the dirt from his knee. He took each kid by the hand again, and they walked the rest of the way to Diamond 2.

"Do we trust him? Completely!" said Miguel, smiling.

EPILOGUE

Two weeks later, Miguel and Claudia were in the playground at Christie Pits. They were looking for Alejandro. But this time, it was a game of hide-and-seek.

"There he is!" shouted Claudia. She pointed to a tree Alejandro was crouching behind.

Miguel looked past Alejandro. Then he gasped.

"Dad!" he shouted.

"Daddy!" Claudia yelled.

A tall man was striding toward the playground. It was their father. When he reached Claudia, he pulled her up and twirled her around. He kissed her cheek as Alejandro shyly joined them.

"I was going to wait until you were finished babysitting. But I just had to see you," their father said to Miguel. "I just came in from the airport."

Miguel waved to his mother, who was standing near a yellow taxi at the top of the hill.

Miguel stared at his father's face. It was like looking

in a mirror. They had the same eyes, the same hair. And the same bright, wide smile.

Miguel's father embraced him and held him tight. When he finally let him go, he held Miguel out at arm's length.

"Thank you," he said softly. There were tears in his eyes. "You've done so much — worked so hard."

"It was all worth it," choked Miguel, his arms around his father again. He looked around the Pits.

"Welcome home, Dad," he said. "Welcome home."

ACKNOWLEDGEMENTS

Kat Mototsune is my editor at Lorimer, and I'm grateful not only for her expertise and her encouragement, but also her friendship. Kat, you are a gem.

Mélanie Raymond, Commissaire at the Immigration and Refugee Board of Canada, generously gave of her time to help me understand the realities of emigrating to Canada from El Salvador. She also told me about many compassionate immigration lawyers she has known who work hard to help new Canadians.

Jaime Estrada taught me a lot about life in El Salvador. Thank you for your smart insights and your understanding of what I was trying to achieve with this book.

Carolyn, as always, for being an integral member of the Blues' coaching staff — as well as their most enthusiastic cheerleader.

Thank you to the Toronto Playgrounds baseball league, whose home field is Christie Pits. They let me launch the first book, *Tagged Out*, in the Pits, overlooking the very diamond where the book was set, during a home-run derby. It was an incredible experience that I will never forget. Thank you to the generous and talented staff and volunteers, including Steve Smith, Paul Hum, Paul Bagnell and Bill Evans. And thank you to all the players and parents who are, after all, at the heart of this baseball story.

Cathie and Katie, always, for your baseball advice, and to Katie for lending your name to a hard-hitting baseball player who embodies your fierce, athletic spirit.

The real-life Coach Coop, for once again letting me use his name, and for being an awesome coach and a great person.

Thanks to Toronto City Councillors Joe "Beau Maverick" Mihevc and Mike "Spike Leighton" Layton, for all they do to support their communities and baseball in Toronto.

And Sally Keefe Cohen, for reminding me to follow my heart about sticking with the Blues.

Also to the baseball parents I've known for years, including Arne, Debra, Stacy, Chris, Mike, Brad, Terry and many others who answered endless baseball questions from me, gave me encouragement and support when I was writing in the hotel lobbies during baseball tournaments, and who protected me and my laptop from fly balls when I wrote in the bleachers.

There's a lot of real baseball in *Sliding Home*. As much, in fact, as I could pack into it. When the young players get advice, it's usually from a real-life baseball coach or a player (like elite catcher, Ryan, who offered some drills). My son Bennett is an elite pitcher and an umpire, and he put most of the words in the umpire's mouth. He also invented Mudball, which I hope becomes an actual thing at the Pits. He played for more than seven years at Christie Pits and still umps there to this day. Also, thank you to all the coaches (including pitching coaches Graham Tebbit and Army Armstrong) and the players who helped to make the Blues — and I hope you, the reader — better at the game of baseball.

My beta readers: WTW — Sue, Ann, Michele, Heather, Andrea, Leslie, Nancy, Debbie, Pam and Beth. And Bennett, Andrew, Val, Angela Misri, Carolyn, Mélanie, Jaime, Katie, Laura Duncan, Patti, Cathie, Gord Enright and Jose.

Thank you to my amazing writing groups, Writers 6 and the very fierce #write-o-rama — thanks for having my back.

A special thank-you to the wonderful Kevin Sylvester, who loves the game of baseball almost as much as Sebastian. Thanks for our baseball chats and for your encouragement.

I'd also like to thank the many booksellers who got to know the Blues and helped spread the word, including